Sherlock Holmes
The Oxford Don

A Sherlock Holmes

Resurgent Mystery

J. B. Varney

Copyright © 2023 J. B. Varney

All rights reserved.

ISBN: 9798390778166

WHAT THEY'RE SAYING

Compelling Story!
Varney's story is an exciting and well written conclusion to the tragedy of the Baskerville legacy. A must read for SH fans.

5.0 out of 5 stars
Reviewed in the US

DEDICATION

To Randy Varney

Who, for the pure love of adventure, explored America's Great Plains with me as a boy.

"The game is... still afoot!"

This book is printed in Baskerville Old Face.

The Sherlock Holmes Resurgent Mystery Series

Book 6

"The game is... still afoot."

J. B. Varney is the 21st Great-Grandson of Fearchar, son of Finley, a lineal descendant of the Thanes of Ross and Moray, who became Chief of Clan Finley in 1236. The Clan held lands in Aberdeenshire and was a member of the Clan Chattan Confederation.

Through his 18th Great-Grandmother, Anne DeGreystoke (born in 1412), he is descended from the line of the Greystoke Barons, her father being John DeGreystoke, 4th Baron Greystoke. Through Anne's mother, Elizabeth de Ferrers, who was herself the Great-Granddaughter of Edward III, King of England, Mr. Varney is descended from the Plantagenet Line.

Contents

Chapter 1 – The Missing Mentor 2

Chapter 2 – Hard Fought! 22

Chapter 3 – The Opening Gambit 40

Chapter 4 – The King's Castle 57

Chapter 5 – Thespian Talents 73

Chapter 6 – The Golden Pince-Nez 95

Chapter 7 – The Darkness 114

Chapter 8 – The Matchstick Message 132

Chapter 9 – Devilish! 153

Chapter 10 – Lincolnshire Wheat 170

Chapter 11 – Move Against Move 184

Chapter 12 – Checkmate 205

Chapter 13 – The Dying Man 220

"There are some trees, Watson, which grow to a certain height, and then suddenly develop some unsightly eccentricity. You will see it often in humans."
                                                   Sherlock Holmes

Chapter 1 – The Missing Mentor

Malcolm Findley, lecturer, tutor, and professor at Christ Church, Oxford, had graduated twenty odd years earlier with first classes in both Classical Moderations and in Literae Humaniores. He was widely considered the most impressive classic scholar of his equally remarkable class, from which several men attained sterling reputations, high offices, and important positions. Despite his strange appearance which included his over-large half-bald dome of a head with its trailing mane of silver-white hair and his golden pince-nez eyeglasses he was an intellectual colossus. This fact must be understood at the outset or little that follows will make any sense. It must also be understood that Oxford College has been chosen as a substitute for the actual institution where these events took place. As the reason for this will no doubt become obvious in the following pages I will say no more about it here.

Because of his many accomplishments Professor Findley had been sought out by several other prestigious colleges and universities to fill positions as Professor of Greek, of Latin, and of Humanities, but he remained quite content to stay on at Christ Church, Oxford. As his reputation continued its continued upward climb, even the "chairs" of several departments at esteemed colleges were soon in the offing.[1] Still, he chose to remain at Christ Church as lecturer, tutor, and professor, an Oxford Don.[2]

This man had in earlier years been a tutor to a much younger Sherlock Holmes and the two had shared a mutual respect for each other. My friend had spoken to me only twice about the Oxford Don

---

[1] "Chairs" is a general term for "chairman" or leader of an educational department at most colleges or universities.

[2] A "Don" is a title of esteem which originated with the Latin "Dominus," the term for "master." A Don was a tutor, fellow, and professor during this period, at Oxford, Cambridge, and Trinity College Dublin. A "fellow" was a member of an elite group of teachers at colleges and universities.

before our unexpected visitors arrived one fine day, it was in early June of '86 as I recall, when there came a ring at our bell.

We looked at each other as if to ask, "Are you expecting someone?" but it was clear from our expressions that neither of us had anything on for the day.

Our page and boy-of-all-chores, Billy, soon came hurrying in with a gentleman's calling card and Holmes stiffened noticeably when he looked at it. This was a strange sight for me as I had seen him greet all manner of nobility from across Europe and even our own Prime Minister with barely a flutter and here he was. He nodded to Billy and the boy disappeared in silence.

"Henry George Liddell," said he quietly without looking up, as he handed the card across.

"Liddell?" I snapped. "That is his book in the cabinet, just there behind your shoulder!" I cried.

The book in question was in fact an 1855 first edition of Liddell's impressive volume entitled, "The History of Rome."

"This is the man of whom Sydney Smith had so famously said, 'that no power on earth, save and except the Dean of Christ Church, should induce him to believe something or other,' the specifics of which I forget."[3]

Holmes simply nodded and I realized my old friend had once again returned, who after all was Henry George Liddell to him.

---

[3] Sydney Smith, English writer, wit, and church cleric.

HENRY GEORGE LIDDELL
DEAN, CHRIST CHURCH OXFORD

I rose while he remained seated and soon the man entered, all six-foot of him, undiminished by age or girth, and followed by an amiable looking assistant with a vacant smile and a grizzled beard.

"You will excuse my calling without notice I hope, Mr. Holmes," he said to my friend, then he turned and stared at me.

"Dr. John Watson," Holmes said.

"Ah," the man said, reaching out to shake my hand, "an honor Sir," said he sincerely. "This is my assistant, Robert Gracefield-Loveday."

"Just Loveday is fine, Gentlemen," the man said as he half bowed.

"Please," I said, gesturing to the settee.

Once we were all seated it was the Dean who spoke first and I could hear the concern in his voice.

"We are in such difficulty Mr. Holmes!"

"Indeed," Holmes almost bristled, "but perhaps you could simply tell me when the Don disappeared and any of the facts you noticed afterward."

J. B. Varney

The Oxford Don

Both men stared in stunned silence and I, who was more used to my friend's puzzling ways, tried to figure out how he had come to his deductions.

"Two days ago Mr. Holmes," the Dean replied, "and the only thing that looks unusual is something written out upon his chalk board. A line which none of us is familiar with or were able to make sense of."

Here the revered educator nodded at his eager assistant and he handed Holmes a small card.

"This is everything?" Holmes demanded as he raced to the table and pulled out a notebook, "every mark and not just the letters."

"Well, I believe so," Dean Liddell answered.

"Yes, it is Mr. Holmes," Loveday replied.

Rome, gone now − a slash from

We all rose and went and gathered around the table, curious as to what Holmes might be up to. His pencil raced across the sheet, up and down, with numbers everywhere. It made no sense to me but I did get my first glimpse at the message.

"It appeared to be a general reference to Roman History," Dean Liddell said.

"It is nothing of the kind," Holmes snapped impatiently. "It is a code Gentlemen; did none of you see that at once? Watson, would you be so good as to hand me down my Visscher?[4] I need to check the latitude and longitude."

---

[4] Nicolas Visscher "New Map of England," published by John Overton, London, England.

"We didn't know what to do Mr. Holmes," Loveday admitted, "so we came to you."

"After two days!" Holmes said pointedly, as he continued his mathematical problem.

"Can you explain the code Sir," Dean Liddell said unhappily. He was not used to being scolded and didn't take such things well.

"It is one of the most elementary of codes," Holmes muttered as he totalled numbers and circled sums. "The English alphabet has 26 letters. By assigning each letter with the numerical value related to their placement in the alphabet we arrive at a numerical equation for each word. Take the word 'slash' for instance. The 's' has a numerical value of 19, the 'l,' a value of 12, the 'a,' of course, is 1, and so forth. Adding all of the values for the word gives us a total of 59 for the word."

"Yes, but where does that get us?" the Dean asked.

Holmes finished the math on the last word, "from," and then wrote out each number under the words corresponding to them on the card.

"Rome, gone now - a slash from"
51   41   53 - 1   59   52

"It gets us precisely here," Holmes said, his finger flying across his Visscher's map of England from right to left and placing a mark and then from bottom to top and placing a second mark.

Six words, six figures, two coordinates. The first is always the latitude, that is from north to south on the globe. 51 degrees, 41 minutes, 53 seconds. The second is longitude, that is east or west. 1 degree, 59 minutes, 52 seconds. The dash represents a 'minus' sign. Everything he wrote on that board was vital, as the minus makes the longitudinal coordinate a negative number."

"Which means it must be somewhere to the west of Greenwich," I said.

"Correct, we calculate to the west of the Prime Meridian with a negative," Holmes said as he took a ruler and drew a line north to south from the mark he'd made on the map. "Where these two lines cross," he murmured almost to himself, as he drew the second line east to west from the line.

"Cirencester!" Dean Liddell exclaimed in shock. "Cirencester! What does that mean?"

"It's actually a point slightly southwest, in the countryside, and that's where we'll find our Oxford Don or the identity of his abductor at minimum," said he with satisfaction.

As he raced for his bedroom, leaving our guests to stare in wonder at his calculations and at the map, he cried out.

"Pack a bag Watson and bring your revolver, for I assure you that this is a dark, ugly business my friend."

We took two cabs to the station, urging them to all possible speed, and shortly we were traveling on the same line west which had brought the university men in earlier.

Once we were settled in, the Dean asked how Holmes had known that Professor Findley was missing.

"It was elementary," Holmes said. "For the Dean of Christ Church College Oxford to arrive at our door unannounced, as you said, you have to admit it an extraordinary thing."

We all agreed.

"But if it were murder, the Police would have been your destination, not Sherlock Holmes. If the deed had been done some time ago and you were coming to me because of your dissatisfaction with them, then I surely would have read about it in the papers long before now. As I haven't and you are here seeking my help, he must have vanished."

"You really are everything that Professor Findley said you were, Mr. Holmes," the Dean announced.

"Did you have reason to doubt him, for in my experience he is the most literal man I've known. Next to Dr. Watson of course."

Holmes comparison of me to his old mentor and tutor was an irony not lost upon me or apparently on the others for that matter, for we all laughed.

"That business with the incomplete sentence though, that was magical Mr. Holmes, no doubt about it," Robert Gracefield-Loveday said.

"Six words," Holmes said. "What message could six words intimate, any six words, but only six?"

"Well, as we've just seen," I replied, "longitude and latitude, but little else."

"Very true Watson."

"But how could you be sure Mr. Holmes, that it wasn't simply a sentence he was writing out for a lesson," the Dean asked.

"For the simple presence of the dash mark, or the minus sign if you will. If you were writing out a sentence for one of your classes, why would you replace one of the words with a minus sign?"

"Remarkable," the Dean said.

"The first three words represented a positive number, obviously. The second three were preceded by the minus sign. If it were a simple sentence then no doubt it would have read, 'Rome, gone now by a slash from...her own hand, perhaps. He needed a word with a value of 59 remember, for the middle coordinate in the second set, and he had only seconds to work. 'Stab' would not do. Then he lit upon slash, a word with exactly the value he required. The minus sign was the key. He put it there to let me know he'd been taken and either where he was being held, at least initially, or a location which would supply me with the identify his captor."

"So you really think he's been abducted Mr. Holmes?" Loveday asked.

"Indeed," Holmes replied, "such a man does nothing rashly."

"But how could he know he should write out a code in the first place Holmes?" I asked. "Surely he didn't know he'd be taken when he was."

"Clearly he saw his fate coming upon him," Holmes remarked, "but only just. He only had mere seconds to leave his message and it presented the secondary challenge of having to appear just as it would if it were simply a sentence he was writing out for a lesson, as Dean Liddell surmised it might be. So, there was either a window with a view of the grounds or a long hallway down which Professor Findley had a view. Which was it Gentlemen?"

"A window," Loveday answered in obvious surprise, "it looks across the quad and might have given him a couple minutes warning, now that you mention it Mr. Holmes."

"Are you telling me that he created that code and came up with a way to disguise it in so short a time Holmes?" I asked in disbelief.

"Yes," my friend said simply. "Such is his mind."

"Then...he knew his kidnapper," Dean Liddell said, suddenly realizing that this crime which had occurred on the college grounds had been conducted by someone he very well might know himself. "He knew him so well..."

"That's correct," Holmes replied. "He knew him so well and he was so aware of the animosity which lay between him and his abductor that just seeing the man was enough to drive him to create the code."

"Mr. Holmes, there is no doubt that what you've shared with us describes the most extraordinary thing I've heard in my long life, but for the sake of argument, just how did the Professor know we could decipher his code?" Loveday asked.

"He didn't, it was that simple. His main hope in writing it out was that there would be at least one person from among all of those who would see the sentence on his chalkboard who would find it puzzling and would record it. That was the most tenuous point of the process for him. He knew if there was such a person that sooner or later I would be contacted."

"Then he knew you could decipher it?" Loveday asked.

"Yes and I'm certain he hoped I'd be contacted sooner than later."

"But why would he assume we'd contact you?" Robert Gracefield-Loveday asked.

"Because anyone who'd been at Christ Church long would recall that he had been my tutor, even if just for a short time."

"Although you were only with us for Michaelmas and Hilary Terms, Mr. Holmes, you were with us and we are all proud of your accomplishments."[5]

---

[5] Oxford has 3 terms: Michaelmas from October-December, Hilary from January-March, and Trinity from April-June.

"One thing I'm still not in the clear on Mr. Holmes. For the Professor to know the location his captor would take him..." Mr. Loveday said.

"We must remember," Holmes cautioned, "that the location may not be where the Professor is, but the ownership of the land will at least identify his captor for us. From that the man who up to now has remained invisible to you will be known and a search may then be launched."

"That was brilliant of him," I said.

"My point is, Mr. Holmes, that the Professor must have known his abductor very well indeed to be able to calculate the location of the man's home so quickly."

"Exactly. I have no doubt that this man is a longtime acquaintance and either a colleague or a former colleague. I can go farther and say that I suspect this man to be a former friend of Professor Findley, someone he once would have visited freely and someone with whom he has since had a harsh falling out. As Oxford is the Professor's world and each college is very much a family, I would believe that you two gentlemen might even be able to give me the name of the man right now, if you were willing and so inclined."

Dean Liddell looked at Robert Loveday clearly intimating that no disclosure should be made.

"Anything we might propose would be pure speculation Mr. Holmes," the Dean said, "mere conjecture, and as such it would in fact likely be counterproductive to your efforts."

"I've solved a hundred of the most tangled mysteries you could imagine Dean Liddell. How many have you solved?"

"Few enough to be sure, but that isn't my field of endeavor is it?"

"No, it is mine though. So when I ask and am met with poorly conceived excuses that, I assure you, is counterproductive. So I will ask you again, with whom has Professor Findley had such a falling out for surely the number cannot be so large that you have difficulty remembering?"

Holmes manner toward the Dean of Christ Church College had been brusque from the start. Beginning with his refusal to stand and shake hands. From this I gathered that there was some history between the two men of which Holmes had told me nothing. This latest contretemps had ruffled the Dean significantly.[6]

"There was a man Mr. Holmes, from before my time though you understand," Loveday offered, "but I've heard enough to say that the two men were great friends in their early years and had a most caustic falling out. So much so that the one left Oxford altogether, while the other remained."

"And his name?"

"Fitzwilliam DeGreystoke of Grimthorpe."

"But you know nothing of the details?"

"No Sir," Loveday replied.

With that Holmes eyes moved to Dean Liddell once again.

"Surely there can be no advantage gained in repeating gossip," the great educator said.

"Have you not yet realized that Oxford has lost its leading Don?" Holmes snapped impatiently. "What I took to be simply poor judgment on your part, Dean Liddell, begins to look like obfuscation. When the policemen asks a witness for information the person is rarely allowed to lean upon such pretexts as not wanting to repeat gossip."

---

[6] Contretemps: quarrel, disagreement, argument.

"You are little changed over all these years Mr. Holmes," the man retorted sharply.

"I might observe the same of you Dean Liddell, but what are such thoughts when set against the life of Professor Malcolm Findley?"

"Perhaps you are right in this instance and I'm being overcautious regarding their private lives."

"I can tell you that if you continue to care so much for their private lives, then one of them may very well lose his actual life if he has not already done so! Now, most murders stem from love or money and sometimes position or fame, but most often love or money, as the author says.[7] Regardless, our friend has not been kidnapped for any but the darkest of purposes. So I will insist that you disclose what you know without further delay."

Holmes' words seemed to sober the august college man markedly.

"There was a young woman," the Dean admitted reluctantly. "Amitas Wycliffe-Ward was a lovely girl and she grew into a beautiful woman. She was the youngest daughter of our university's Chancellor. Her family called her 'Queenie' for her regal air. She had beauty, wealth, and intelligence and so had every expectation of the greatest of marriages, but Findley wouldn't be discouraged. What that man lacked in fortune, birth, stature, and good looks, he more than made up for in aggressive determination. He was an acclaimed Oxford Don even in those early days and believed that this alone was enough to carry him across the finish to the blue riband. You may remember that his hair had turned prematurely white even when you were with him."

Holmes nodded with a smile of remembrance.

"He was ever the most fiercely independent of men," Holmes recalled, "and once he took a thing into his mind he would not release it."

"Yes, quite, that is one way of describing him," the Dean said, mysteriously. "The other man was Fitzwilliam DeGreystoke of Grimthorpe. He was a man almost the opposite of Professor Findley, being

---

[7] "For love or money," a saying first used in novel form in the book "Castle Rackrent," by Maria Edgeworth, published by J. Johnsons of London, ©1801.

of high birth, a descendant of the noteworthy Greystoke Barons of Greystoke and Grimthorpe and was due to inherit a quarter share in money and lands, all of which he has in the years since taken possession of. In that regard he had the best start of the two, off the line so to speak, but he was just as short and diminutive as Professor Findley and he too was far from handsome, as you may recall."

"He was the dark-haired Fellow, with that wild something about the eyes?" Holmes asked.

"Quite so and not someone the beautiful Amitas Wycliffe-Ward was likely to choose for her Prince Charming, even if her father had approved, which he had not. Still, DeGreystoke saw that Professor Findley was pressing his suit with so little cause for hope that he felt himself by far the better choice in a two-horse race. So it began."

"And did neither man have, that is, did they not realize such a girl would want a strapping, handsome fellow?" I asked.

"I'm afraid that in the rarified world of academia Dr. Watson, we find it very easy to inflate the value of the mind over that of the merely physical. Mankind's brute nature is set at odds against our higher self. Although neither man was a likely Romeo they still believed they should be considered by the beautiful Juliet in our play. It never occurred to either of them, I believe, that a woman who was their equivalent for appearance would never stand a chance at catching a Romeo for herself."

"And what did Miss Wycliffe-Ward decide?" Holmes asked.

"After a prolonged debut during which she seemed to favor Professor Findley and reveled in all the attention and gifts showered upon her by several suitors, her father insisted she settle upon August Osborn, one of the three heirs of the vast Somerset Osborn Fortune, all 6' 2" and 14 stone of him.[8] He was a scrumhalf on our rugby team in fact.[9] We defeated Cambridge that year you know, largely on the strength of those Osborn legs of his too," the Dean said, contradicting his words about valuing the mind over the physical, at least for the moment.

"So she obeyed her father and married the handsome lad after all," I said knowingly.

"By no means Dr. Watson. I cannot say if the young woman had found true love or if there was a degree of rebelliousness involved in going against her noble father's wishes, but she selected Professor

---

[8] One stone = 14 lbs. so 14 stone = 196 lbs.
[9] Scrumhalf is a back position directly behind the scrum.

Findley in the end and they've been one of the happiest couples in our college, if all the signs are to be trusted."

"So Fitzwilliam DeGreystoke was turned down," Holmes remarked.

"And the man took it very hard Mr. Holmes. It was almost to the degree of a personal affront. Then to make matters even worse he was beaten out for the only Christ Church position which was likely to come open for several years and a position DeGreystoke had fully assumed was already his. All in all it was the final blow and I can't say I was happy when he moved on."

"So this came down to both love and money," I said, looking at Holmes.

"And this is our man Gentlemen, our abductor," Holmes announced, "Fitzwilliam DeGreystoke."

Dr. John H. Watson, MD

Chapter 2 – Hard Fought!

"You are a wonder Mr. Holmes; I confess this was all a jumble to my mind and you've cleared matters up," Dean Liddell said, in his most earnest expression yet, as he and Gracefield-Loveday rose to depart the train in Oxford. "I wish you good luck upon your journey and pray you will inform us whenever you can, as we will be waiting eagerly for any word."

"A pleasure to meet you both," Loveday said as he stepped out.

"The formalities now having been duly observed Watson, we can now get on with the business at hand."

"You were a little hard on the Dean, I thought."

"Was I?" Holmes said, distractedly, "I hadn't noticed." Then a guilty grin told me he was fully aware of what he'd done. "You've noticed, have you not Watson, that the more high and worthy these people believe themselves, the less I am inclined to bend myself to their inflated self-estimations. It has ever been so with me, I'm afraid. In this my brother Mycroft was blessed with the happier personality, for he can contentedly stoop to kiss royal rings all day long and count himself the luckiest of lads."

Holmes had shared similar comments with me over our years together but this was the most concise and personal explanation he'd ever supplied me.

"You are among the most fiercely independent of men," I acknowledged, repeating the words he'd just spoken regarding his old mentor.

"Now," said he, ignoring my words completely, "to our business."

"The rescue of Professor Findley," I replied.

"I wish matters were as clean as I've made them look to our university friends Watson. I confess my good fellow, that I very much fear we are far from finished with this business. I expect this to be a most hard fought and ugly thing before we reach the end."

"Why do you say so Holmes? For this is not the first time you've made use of that word 'ugly' in reference to this case."

"As to my use of that word, this is a personal vendetta very much like the ones we expect to read of in the more sensational rags with regard to Italy or Sicily in particular. It seems strange to find it in the cooler blood of an Englishman of Fitzwilliam DeGreystoke's ilk, of all things, but there you have it. As to why this will be so hard fought a thing, I am surprised at you Watson, for you are a sporting man and I fully expected you to recall that name."

"Recall...what name?" I asked, confused, for other than the passing mention of Rugby we hadn't touched upon sport all day.

"Fitzwilliam DeGreystoke."

"Fitzwilliam DeGreystoke," I repeated, for I still had no clue what Holmes might be referring to.

"The National Chess Championship last year Watson? You won a sizeable bet against your old school chum, Stamford, did you not?"

"Of course," I cried, wondering how I could have forgotten so unique a name as DeGreystoke. "So that's the devil who has your old tutor."

"And that's why this will be a hard-fought thing! And thanks to Dean Liddell we already start from behind," Holmes said, clearly unhappy. "You took it that I jested when I compared you to Malcolm Findley, Watson. All of you did, but I assure you my good fellow, I was in deadly earnest. There is no steadier soul upon our island lest it be you and how would I react if you vanished of a morning without a single word? Would I wait two days to begin my search. How Dean Liddell justifies his actions has always been an instructive exercise in self-delusion and protectionism. For an intelligent man he has the most shocking lack in judgment and instinct I've ever encountered. Had it not been for Gracefield-Loveday, we would have gotten nothing. To simply assume that his leading Don, as sure a man as there is ever likely to be, had just determined to take to the hills upon a walking tour of Windemere or some other equally distant place, without bothering to say a word of it even to his wife, and to delay notifying anyone for 48 hours, it's unconscionable! I can't imagine how Professor Findley's wife must have taken all this. Such a failure of judgment."

Holmes' words of praise for me had not escaped my notice and to be compared with a man like

Professor Findley made for some grand thoughts indeed. I had heard little enough from Holmes about the Oxford Don, but what I had heard had been of the most glowing terms. To hear Holmes' estimation of the Dean of Christ Church College, however, was nothing short of revelatory.

"And to give a man like DeGreystoke such an advantage…"

My friend's words faded away as he retreated once again into that secret world of his inner thoughts and I contented myself with watching the scenery pass by in the dimming light of early evening.

I don't know how long I'd been asleep when I was awakened by Holmes' shaking and stared out at a darkness, illuminated only by the gas lamps.

"Cirencester," Holmes muttered, "center of the ancient Romans."

When I stepped out upon the platform I was hit with a bracing night chill and pulled my suit jacket close around me.

Holmes was already at the end of the platform waving for me and as I hurried on I marveled at the man's energy. There were times when I almost believed him an automaton who required no sleep at all to function.

"This good man has volunteered to deliver us to the very spot off the Tetbury Road," Holmes said, pointing at the weather-etched station master.

"It will save ye Gen'almen time in finding a cart and then there's the cost, and as it is but a quarter mile off my way home. The missus will not mind."

We climbed into the man's little jaunting cart as he lit a single lantern affixed to the dashboard.[10] I sat opposite Holmes behind our driver as the old horse jerked us suddenly into a slow if steady motion.

---

[10] Dashboard: originally a board or leather shield suspended on metal rods and placed between the driver and the horse. Its purpose was to keep the driver safe and clean when the horse was at the trot and throwing clods of dirt or mud up behind it. In time it became an actual extension of the cart body itself.

"Are they expectin' ye out at Dryman's?" the man asked after little more than a mile.

"They are," Holmes replied, "but we still want to surprise them so if you would be so good as to let us off at the turning."

"Aye but mind their lane in the dark. We've had a fair bit o' rain this spring and the ruts are all full o' water."

At the lane we stepped down and thanked the man and Holmes handed him a sovereign for his troubles.

"A pleasant evening to you then," said he, with only his teeth shining brightly in the moonlight.

"Dryman House then, is that it?" I asked as we trudged down the narrow lane that cut across the fields and passed the lonely place along its course.

"That's it Watson but I had to be careful not to give our game away. Before you joined us on the platform he told me a certain Merridew was the manager, although no one lives permanently at the old place."

"So any light will declare their presence."

At that moment there was an odd commotion ahead of us in the darkness and with only a pale moon shrouded in clouds, the sound was our first clue we had that a man on horseback was retreating at a gallop.

"They posted a guard Watson!" Holmes cried as he took off at full tilt in a burst of speed that would have impressed any collegiate runner. The quickly fading shadow of the horseman was soon swallowed up in a dark copse of trees in the distance and even

Holmes thin form became blended into the veil of darkness. I fell farther behind with each stride but I pressed on for another half mile before the copse became distinguishable as a rambling two-storied brick affair amid a grove of mature trees surrounded by a thick hedge which was trimmed to chest height.

There was no sign of Holmes, the horseman, nor anyone else for that matter, but light could be seen at an open door and an upstairs window of the old manse.

I hobbled into the grounds through a gate itself covered over in hedge and trimmed in neat curves. A long byre stood off to the right and back from the road but the house itself loomed up high in the old style of the great country houses which had once been the de rigueur for the wealthy.[11]

As I approached the door, leaning hard upon my cane, Holmes came flying out, wide-eyed and with every nerve on alert.

"The birds have all flown," he fairly shouted as he launched himself across the broad lawn toward the dark hulk of the byre, where only a dim ray of light escaped through a partially opened door.

When I entered I found my friend bent over some machine in the byre's central alley, pouring gasoline.

"Holmes?" I said, intimating a question as to what he might be doing, but then my eyes adjusted. "I say," I declared, "do you know what that is?"

---

[11] De rigueur: something necessitated by the social customs and practices of the day.

"A contraption which I very much hope will soon close the distance between me and our prize," said he as he replaced the lid and tied the fuel can on with a length of rope.

"That's a Daimler-Maybach riding-cycle, Model 'B,' I'd say from the sloped front armature," I muttered excitedly, "if I'm correct."[12]

I'd read about the invention and had awaited its arrival in England but had lost track of it in the business of life and now it was out and in a second model even.

With that Holmes pulled hard on a cord and the little engine popped into life, spurting exhaust in little puffs until it got going well.

"Bring the horse and follow up Watson," said he, pointing to an old plough horse no doubt grandfathered to the farm.

With some further adjustments to dials and switches the engine was soon puttering respectably and with the tip of his hat my friend was off into the darkness, careening off at a surprising speed.

I coughed in the cloud of exhaust and stared dubiously at the giant animal in the last stall but one. Despite Holmes' wishes I knew it was futile to chase after him upon the brave old steed and taking the lantern I returned to the house.

An hour later I could hear the sputtering of the machine returning from its adventure.

---

[12] Gottlieb Daimler and Wilhelm Maybach developed their "reitwagon" or riding car in the 1880's, releasing what is now viewed as the first motorcycle in 1885. Daimler is considered the father of the motorcycle.

My own thought was that Holmes was returned too soon to have overtaken the carriage and horseman and disposed of the blackguards to the police and the victim to the hospital or a hotel, so they'd given him the slip. However, when he entered the sitting room his expression was one of elation.

He flopped down in one of the chairs which faced the fire and stretched out his long legs.

"I'm chilled to the bone," he declared, ignoring the subject at hand. "I say Watson, what did you call that, a riding cycle?"

"It's a German-built Daimler-Maybach, gasoline powered, belt-driven, riding-cycle," I replied.

"Well," Holmes said, thoughtfully, "there's a future for that machine if my experience is anything to go by, for despite the lead they had amassed on me by the time I got going it was barely enough to escape me."

"But it was enough...to escape you?"

"Just enough Watson. That machine had closed the gap admirably I tell you."

"But Holmes," I declared, confused, "if they escaped you, why are you so pleased?"

"Do you remember one of the first lessons you learned Watson, after we met? I believe it was in reference to the Goulden-Pankhurst Pearl Necklace Case. The thief had escaped the police but instead of leaving the country he stayed to enjoy himself."

"And you found him in Farringdon, not far from the Smithfield Meat Market."

"Precisely and what did the man, Reynolds, do when he noticed us trailing?" Holmes asked, still in his highly excited state.

"He went into the maze of buildings there at Charterhouse Square, the school as I recall, or was it the almshouse? I know it was just around the corner from Barts."[13]

"Right you are Watson and what did I say at the time? Do you recall?"

"We have him now, Dr. Watson! Or something to that effect," I quoted.

"And the lesson?"

---

[13] "Barts," the nickname for St. Bartholomew's Hospital, where Watson and Holmes first met in Sir Arthur Conan Doyle's "A Study in Scarlet," published 1887.

"If you're on the run you should never go into a tall building, but if you do, never go up, where your entrapment is inevitable."

"Well done Watson! You may go through but never up."

"Up leads only to your inevitable death or capture," I said, repeating the words I'd heard some six years earlier.

"We caught him, George Marcel Reynolds, the fugitive surgeon because he went up. We returned the pearls and received acclaim."

"And a large reward as I recall."

"Yes, quite a large reward," Holmes agreed. "And now I'll add to that lesson. When you're in the west country, never take a terminal line farther west into the remote reaches which lie amidst a great scarp."

"They didn't!" I said, stunned. "That means they went and landlocked themselves up there along the escarpment."

"Yes my dear fellow, they did. They're now surrounded by the length and breadth of the Cotswold Scarp to the north and west," Holmes confirmed.[14] "Some of the lads of around the station told me that Sheepescombe is the end of that line and the only place with an inn. It was apparently one of the old cloth manufacturing towns back in its heyday but has long been depressed and sparsely populated as a result."

---

[14] The Cotswold Scarp is characterized by a steep slopes falling off of highland ledges into deeply gouged out ravines and valleys. Travel there was a challenge during the Victorian Era.

"You've telegrammed?"

"To Scotland Yard? I did that from Baker Street before we left, and now that they know about the kidnapping of Professor Findley they'll no doubt be sending an inspector. And tonight, from the rail station, I wired the Sheepescombe Constabulary telling them to observe and notify us of the activities of the men. The men are thankfully quite unique in their appearance and traveling together they'll be even more distinct. The milk train is the first one out in the morning, arriving in Cirencester at 6:30."

"But could DeGreystoke not simply hire a cart and disappear overland? After all, he has to know that Sherlock Holmes is waiting for him back in Cirencester doesn't he?"

"Think Watson, could we provide the police any description of the horseman we encountered earlier upon the road?"

"By no means," I confessed.

"And by the same principle neither could the horseman describe us. He was placed as a general warning of any encroachment. I doubt very seriously that DeGreystoke knows who his pursuers are. As his young companion was his only eyes upon the road, he can know even less than we know."

"Why do you call him young, this companion?"

"That machine my good fellow, the Daimler-Maybach, that is most assuredly a young man's machine at this stage in its development, wouldn't you agree. I can assure you that while it did well for speed, it is the most jarring ride a man might find this side of America's Great Plains, where the iron rimmed wheels of the Pioneer wagons have carved out a path through dirt and stone alike. Also, there is the steering to be considered. If the designers of the riding-cycle asked for my own humble opinion I would tell them that it requires broader handlebars thus increasing turning torque. A smaller-to-larger gearing could give the rider additional assistance with turning, but as it now sits, one must be a most fit and active man to manage it safely."

"I suppose it is a leap to imagine Fitzwilliam DeGreystoke at 5' 4" and perhaps 9 stone, handling that monster," I admitted."[15]

"It holds, therefore, Watson, that DeGreystoke has enlisted the help of a younger and stronger ally to aid him in the capture and murder of Professor Findley."

These last words were chilling, bringing as they did the goal of the abduction back into immediate and inescapable clarity.

"So it was to be murder all along?"

"Indeed," Holmes replied. "And if I read it rightly it is to be a slow process."

"But why not kill him immediately? Why risk the chase?"

"With a very few exceptions Watson, the Oxford Dons live on college grounds. Professor Findley certainly did. For most of the faculty, that place is their life. Fitzwilliam DeGreystoke knew his former friend's habits and was forced to abduct him from the college. He couldn't be sure he wasn't seen."

---

[15] 9 stone = 126 lbs.

"So he had to wait to see if anyone had seen him or had deduced he was the mastermind."

"The chess player in him required him to take that step. If he were to be known, far better to face the crime of abduction rather than murder. As it was no one saw him or recognized him if they did. However, Professor Findley did and he had just enough time and wit to scrawl that message on the chalkboard. As circumspect as DeGreystoke was, he clearly didn't recognize the code hidden in the incomplete sentence."

"Or he never would have left it."

"Correct Watson. It was a mistake of immense proportions."

"So now that he knows we're on to him, will he abandon his plan and try to escape?"

"He should. It would be the wise thing to do and but for two factors I don't believe he would have hesitated."

"And what are those factors?"

"The first is, as I told you earlier, that this is a personal matter, a vendetta if you will. It is so far beyond any logic-based game he has ever played that it is difficult to overstate it."

"So DeGreystoke the Chess Champion may not be thinking as clearly as he normally would?"

"That is exactly the case my good fellow. I noted that you recognized an unusual shortness in my manner, even for me, back there when the academians descended upon us from the hallowed grounds of Oxford, with their news."

Grimthorpe - ancestral seat of the de Greystoke Family

"I did," I admitted, "and the speed with which you acted, that was unusual too, even for you."

"Yes, I count you my friend Watson, and the Professor was a trusted mentor. No man is a cold machine, void of feeling, no matter what we tell ourselves. Sherlock Holmes isn't and Fitzwilliam DeGreystoke isn't either. Regardless of what he tells himself, his emotions are at play in his decisions."

"And the second factor."

"Yes, that," said he, mysteriously. "We sit here in one of DeGreystoke's properties, a fine old country house in kept grounds with its own estate manager. How would you describe the furnishings Watson?" he asked.

I had looked around the place while I'd waited for Holmes' return and I looked about the sitting room again.

"Lavish," I said, "just as one would expect from such a country house."

"Old money then?"

"Indeed," I agreed, "and no struggles."

By this last comment I meant, of course, that Fitzwilliam DeGreystoke had not suffered with the economic realities of our changing times which had gripped so many of his peers.

"Do you recall when Dean Liddell asked me how I knew Professor Findley had disappeared?"

"Yes, that was a dramatic moment," I said with a smile of satisfaction, for I took pride in even my friend's smallest victories.

"Do you remember my answer?"

"You reasoned that if it were murder you would surely have already read about it in the papers and as you had not, then..."

"Quite so, quite so," Holmes interrupted, still full of the exhilaration he so often felt when he was on the hunt.

"And the same principle applies here as well. If Fitzwilliam DeGreystoke had been preparing for the possibility of fleeing abroad would he not have liquidated his holdings? Would we not have heard of so many old and established estates going on the market? Would he still have access to this country home? And would he not have sold off all the valuable furnishings first, in preparation for his departure, if necessary. His many properties would surely be forfeit after a criminal action, even an unsuccessful one. He would lose another fortune, even if he were able to flee with his accounts. Few men would be so generous would they? And as I have discovered Watson, Grimthorpe, his family seat and his property, remains as it always has."

I nodded; Holmes' deductions had once again amazed me.

"So he's committed to seeing it through despite the fact that he is now pursued?"

"He would have been wise to have taken your counsel Watson, as I said. Had he abandoned Professor Findley here and fled into the night for distant ports it is likely he could have seen his way clear, despite the clarion call of Scotland Yard which has now rung out across England. His deep hatred, however, which has been engendered by so many grievances held on to over the years, has pushed him to play a desperate game unlike any chess game he would ever have allowed himself."

"Apparently it's an all or nothing game as well."

"Even when it develops into a case of double-or-nothing, my good fellow, you see he still remains steadfast."

"And if it comes down to his having to abandon so much of his family's heritage and his wealth?"

"So be it!" Holmes said, "Although I suspect he would never admit such a possibility."

"Why Holmes?"

"His confidence Watson."

"Because he has won so consistently at the highest levels."

"That and the fact that he has been so successful in the field of crime as well," said he, mysteriously.

Chapter 3 – The Opening Gambit

Holmes made himself further at home in the country house and we'd soon finished some fine cucumber sandwiches, a plate of meat and cheese, a bowl of fresh strawberries, and a pot of especially good Chinese Oolong tea. He had hired one of "the lads" in Cirencester to come out with a cart and horse and deliver us back to the city before sunrise and we'd just finished our clean up and doused the lights when the man rolled noisily up before the door and his horse shook his harness.

"I found this wool long coat Watson," said he and it should suit you. As the owner cannot refuse us I recommend you avail yourself of it as the night is quite cold."

"And what of you Holmes?" I asked, for I knew he'd been chilled to the bone by his long ride on the Daimler-Maybach and he'd only just gotten warm again.

"I will make use of this wool blanket," said he, "and I'll be quite comfortable."

After we made our start back to Cirencester the clouds passed, the stars came out brightly, and the air became instantly colder.

"So you have arranged a net around the Scarp?" said I in a whisper, although our driver was his own world, quietly humming familiar tunes to pass the miles.

"I've informed Cirencester and Gloucester as well, which is east of the Scarp, and they've set up checkpoints and been in contact with Scotland Yard. One of the Inspectors should be with us in the morning, although how early is yet to be seen. The milk train will be out early and I suspect this will be the train they attempt to escape on."

"You sound confident."

"If I do Watson, it is a fragile certitude, for we are now up against a true mastermind and the game is afoot."

"But as you said, they took the terminal line west into the Scarp."

"Yes but no one need remind me that we are facing a mind of the first water, Watson.[16]"

---

[16] "Of the first water" – a phase which means to be of the highest quality. It is a reference to the archaic system by which

I shook my head for it seemed to me that in his attempt not to underestimate his adversary, that Holmes had granted DeGreystoke too much credit.

"Do you recall his defeat of Isidor Von Soltesz?"

"The brilliant Hungarian champion...back in '83," said I sadly, "You know I lost five quid on that one."

How well I recalled Stamford's glee as if it were only yesterday. Von Soltesz had been supremely confident going into the match against DeGreystoke and was heavily favored. Holmes merely shook his head at my obvious gloom at the memory of it.

"It was a magnificent countermove that won it. You recall he sacrificed his rook," said he, "and that is the man we're up against now."

"But surely Holmes, the noose is tight about him now with the surrounding constabularies in position and the Yard involved..."

Holmes' expression turned almost pitiful at my words and then I recalled how often he'd given the clearest directions only to be let down by one official group or another. His elation was fading as the eastern horizon began to lighten with coming sunrise.

We waited upon the platform as the whistle of the milk train could be heard in the distance. Then the smoke from her stack could be made out above the trees. Finally, and as if in slow motion, she rolled to a stop and released her steam pressure with a great hiss. Workman turned to the freight cars,

---

diamonds were first rated. The most brilliant and flawless were said to be "of the first water."

unloading the milk cans sent in from surrounding dairies as fast as they could.

There were only a handful of passengers on the early train, as was no doubt usual. One was a young woman, likely a teacher returning from a weekend visit to her family out in one of the villages. She was carrying a carpet bag. A rosy cheeked, elderly couple who looked as if they'd come home from a walking holiday along the Scarp was followed closely by their luggage, and a few others straggled out, none of whom bore the slightest resemblance whatsoever to our fugitives.

The signal was given and a handful of constables rushed onto the train from front to back, searching everywhere anyone might be able to hide away. After a few minutes and one by one they all emerged dejected, the train was empty.

"We found nothing onboard Mr. Holmes," a Detective Inspector who'd introduced himself as Lyman P. Naylor said. He was with the Cirencester Constabulary and was obviously taken with the idea that he was working with the famous Sherlock Holmes, but he seemed to need every new action spelled out for him and his men.

Holmes said nothing but I could tell something momentous was about to happen. He had that look he always got when the thoughts were tumbling one after another in his head like dominoes, a thousand a second as he went through his familiar process of elimination. Something was bothering him and as like as not it was the smallest detail, something in the wrong place, what he referred to as an anomaly.

"It is a thing which doesn't belong in that setting Watson," he'd once explained. "While we see the form of things, the details are merely filled in, glossed over by a conscious mind which refuses to assign its full attention to what the subconscious has already deemed as 'unimportant minutia.' Yet, it is in that minutia where the solutions exist. It is in those revealing details where illumination may be found."

Then I saw those eyes brighten in a flash and that familiar voice called out my name.

"Watson," he cried, as he spun and began his race to the end of the platform, "they just passed us!"

"They?" I called, running after my friend as best I could.

"They? They who?" the Inspector called after us? Then he began calling for his men.

When I rounded the corner and rushed along the street I could see where Holmes stood looking down into the thick verge of brush and shrubs along an alley.

As I closed upon him I heard him mutter, "Two more oddities for Scotland Yard's museum."

By the time I reached his side the young Inspector had caught up with me, putting two strides to each of mine, and together we stared at the two traveling trunks which had only recently passed us behind the elderly couple upon the platform.

"Them?" the Inspector cried.

"The elderly couple was them?" I said in shock.

"No, Gentlemen, the elderly couple was not them," Holmes said, leaving both of us still puzzled.

"Then how was it done Holmes?"

"The young man pushing the hand truck with the trunks on it," he said, as Inspector Naylor's men arrived and began pulling the trunks from the brush.

"What about him?" the Inspector insisted.

"Did you notice he wasn't wearing the railroad's uniform? Then there were the trunks."

"What of the trunks?" I asked.

"How much baggage would an elderly couple take with them on a hiking holiday on the scarp?"

The light dawned upon us simultaneously. Two large trunks as well as the bags they each carried would have been far more than such an excursion could ever possibly have required. As to the man pushing the hand truck, workmen were all over the platform throughout the day. A group of them had emptied the dairy freight cars in fact. His presence would even have been expected, but you would only see a liveried railway employee upon a hand truck bearing a guest's luggage.

"Open the trunk," Holmes directed and when the constable did so we beheld an elaborate deck plate in the bottom.

"What is it Sir?" the constable asked.

"That is a most efficient breathing apparatus," Holmes said, tapping the side of the trunk with his cane. "A dozen large holes were cut into the bottom of each of the trunks," he continued, "then spacers were fixed and a deck was placed above it. Around the edge of this deck half circles were cut out."

"But why Mr. Holmes? Why go to the trouble?"

"Because Inspector, this system allows superior airflow through the trunk without putting limbs and fingers at risk of injury. The air may enter but the parts of the body can't reach any of the air holes and suffer injury. Now, if you look under these two reinforcement slats on the lids I think you'll find that each has been raised by a quarter of an inch. Underneath each of the slats dozens of air exit ports were drilled, corresponding to the strange rows of holes on the inside of each lid, then the slat was replaced above spacers."

"Making the holes invisible to the naked eye," I said, "while allowing the hot air to leave the trunk."

"A quite unique method of transporting people," Holmes admitted with a degree of admiration.

"Surely the kidnapped man would have cried out, or was he gagged, I suppose?"

"More likely sedated," said I, "as even gagging a man cannot silence him."

"Well done Watson, for a conscious man might kick the side of the trunk with the toe of his shoe or knock with his fist, even if his hands and ankles were bound, and one can hum surprisingly loudly," Holmes remarked, "as I've found recently."

"Let me understand this," Inspector Naylor said earnestly, "the elderly couple was not a part of the plot?"

"They might easily have been hired to act as if the trunks were theirs," Holmes replied, "and to walk out with the young man close behind. Even if this were the case, such an act could hardly have seemed questionable to them. It might even have been explained away easily enough as a joke being played upon some pal of the young man. For a few shillings Professor DeGreystoke, through the efforts of his accomplice, could have secured a plausible cover to further secure his activity. Either way, the elderly couple were not intimate with either DeGreystoke or his crime. They would still be worth investigating, Inspector, as you might find out more, but their guilt, if it exists, will not be a matter for the courts."

"And the accomplice?" I asked.

"No doubt the man dressed as the worker with the hand truck was also the owner of the Daimler-Maybach riding-machine Watson. Being unknown to us he could move about freely without fear of detection and, as such, he operated as the front man in this operation."

"We'll catch them when they try to leave the city Mr. Holmes," Inspector Naylor said confidently. "I have men posted on the roads and they have the descriptions."

"No doubt your efforts have been noteworthy Inspector Naylor," Holmes said, "but had escape from Cirencester been their immediate goal, surely they would not have exited the trunks, after all, if Dr. Watson is correct at least one of their number is unconscious. No, they've gone to ground within your fine city and whereas you can only keep your men posted for a few hours or a day or two at most, they have the luxury of outlasting you. Then when you pull your officers they will be free to leave without concern. I'm afraid they've got all the advantage upon their side now Inspector. It is an outcome we must expect from a chess master."

"So you've gone and lost them, have you?"

The raucous voice from behind us was familiar somehow and when we turned we found Inspector Lestrade smiling at us, his dark eyes dancing.

"I came as soon as they notified me," said he with a shrug of his shoulders, "and now I've arrived

I find the birds flown. How now Mr. Holmes, this won't do."

"The birds have indeed flown," Holmes said as he shook the man by the hand, "but it is just the opening gambit."

At that moment another constable joined us.

"I brought Constable DeJong with me to help with the case, you remember him don't you Mr. Holmes?"[17]

"Of course, it's good to have you on the case with us Constable," he said, welcoming the young man we'd worked with in a recent case."

"Dr. Watson," said he, offering me his hand.

"How are you Constable?"

"Good now that I'm back working with you two."

I smiled and nodded at this observation.

---

[17] DeJong – pronounced Dee-Yong, of Dutch/German origin.

"You Gentlemen have a way of stirring things up if you don't mind my saying so."

"It does seem to...stir, doesn't it?" then I made the introductions for Inspector Naylor.

"This is Detective Inspector Lyman P. Naylor, Gentlemen, of the Cirencester Constabulary, and Detective Inspector Lestrade," I said. "You've just heard Constable DeJong's name, of the London Metropolitan Police."

"And these are for Scotland Yard's museum," Holmes said, tapping the trunks again and stepping aside so that Inspector Lestrade could get a good view of Professor DeGreystoke's handiwork.

"We wouldn't want that design getting out in public now would we. There'd be no telling what the regular folk might get up to if they saw these."

We adjourned to the Crown Public House for a well-earned breakfast and Inspector Naylor was able to secure a wood-paneled upstairs banqueting room for our privacy.

"What do you know about the accomplice Mr. Holmes," Naylor asked promptly after we'd made our selections.

"5' 11', 170 lbs., green eyes, thin face, short sandy brown hair, exceptionally strong, slightly pigeon-toed, and right-handed. He is also the younger son of a prosperous, established family, was an athlete and likely a sportsman on a university team. He is a seasoned boxer despite his youth and a former student of DeGreystoke at his present school. These are just a few points for now,"

Holmes said, "but it gives us something to go on does it not?"

When he looked up we were all staring at him in wonder. After me, Lestrade was the most used to Holmes incredible abilities, but for the younger men, Inspector Naylor and Constable DeJong, it was all a complete shock. While Lestrade scribbled all the details down in shorthand in his little notebook Inspector Naylor expressed his wonder.

"I've never seen anything like that Mr. Holmes," said he, "but pray, how do you know such things for it seems utterly impossible to pass a man upon a platform and see all that?"

"I knew a blind man once, Inspector Naylor, one Frederick Keneally by name and hailing from the town of Ardsley in Yorkshire. He could tell you more about a person he'd just met than many could who had the gift of sight. How is that possible?"

"I would say that in the absence of sight the man must have developed other skills to help him cope."

"Well said," Holmes replied, "and it proves that our eyes are merely one of the means available to us by which we assess our world. It was easy enough to take in the man's height, weight, eye and hair color, and the shape of his face without doing anything miraculous. It was simply attention to detail, labor if you will, but not magic. As to the deductions which I made upon his strength, his gait, and which was his predominant hand, these also were based upon simple, practiced observation."

"As to the first, his strength, I assure you that it was elementary, as I had just watched the young man lift and place two trunks singlehandedly upon the hand truck and then there was the ease with which he handled the truck itself. No, I can see nothing remarkable in drawing that conclusion."

"As to his gait, one need only familiarize oneself with the characteristics which result from the various impediments. For example, a man with one shorter leg will typically be found to have a gait which logically rises and falls, as if he were riding in a boat upon the waves. Someone who has a turned-in toe or both, pigeon-toed as it is called, will suffer from

The Oxford Don

an increased incidence of stumbling. This is caused by the toe of the effected foot, when in motion, striking the inside arch or ball of set foot. Our man stumbled upon the flat pavement of the platform, dropping a bundle of paperwork between his feet as a result. To deduce that he would pick up the papers with his dominant hand was, mathematically, highly likely."

"It all seems so reasonable when you explain each in its own part," the young Inspector admitted.

"Have I not said so before Watson?"

"Indeed you have," I confessed, "a few times."

"That's all well and good Mr. Holmes, for eye color and being right or left-handed," Inspector Lestrade remarked, "but those other things you came up with, they're another creature altogether and you'll not persuade me otherwise. How did you figure on his being a younger son, a seasoned boxer or, for that matter, a former student of this Professor, from just a sighting upon the platform? That's what I want to know."

"Ah, you've caught me out there Inspector, for I had more data than just a passing upon a rail station platform to go by."

"I'm glad to hear it, otherwise I believe you would have been a leading candidate for those witch trials they got up to in America a few years back."

When Lestrade said a few years back he would have been more correct to have said nearly two hundred years, but I said nothing.

"Yes, quite," Holmes replied vaguely before beginning his fuller explanation. "That he was the son of a prosperous family was based upon his owning the newest model of the Daimler-Maybach riding-cycle which I know from Dr. Watson is imported from Germany. This is not something an even moderately prosperous businessman might afford and yet, here we had a man in his twenties owning and operating it. From this it was a small thing to deduce that he must be from a prosperous family capable of showering such wealth upon their children so that they may spend good portions of it upon such frivolities."

This explanation was met the same impressed expressions from all, save Inspector Lestrade who continued to press him.

"And from an established family?"

"It holds that so noteworthy an Oxford Professor as Fitzwilliam DeGreystoke had been for a season, not to mention an international chess champion, would be hired by another of our country's finest schools as soon as he was available, would you not agree?"

"I would," Lestrade replied.

"It also follows that the young men he would be instructing would reflect the status of their school, as is commonly seen throughout the Kingdom. From this it isn't a difficult equation to determine that DeGreystoke would find his college the prime source from which to recruit his accomplice. The only place more likely would be someone from his own family, but our man had only one brother, a man who never produced a child. DeGreystoke himself never married, although it must be admitted that he tried for the woman who ultimately chose for Professor Findley and this loss only seems to have reinforced his famously retiring nature. It doesn't mean that a family connection is an impossibility, for there is his mother's side of the family to consider, and we must keep the possibility in mind. It does, however, make it highly unlikely that the paternal side of his family could have provided a man of suitable age and abilities."

"You've done it again Mr. Holmes," Lestrade remarked with an air of disappointment. "Try as I might you are deucedly hard to trip up in your reasoning Sir. I was always inclined to put your self-assuredness down to bluster, but I've been wrong."

Holmes nodded his head slightly. It was a small gesture but knowing him as I did, I knew Lestrade's words, especially as they had been delivered in public, were a great personal victory for my friend.

"Mr. Holmes," Constable DeJong said, putting his own question forward, "how was it you realized he wasn't the eldest son and a boxer? Those have me beat."

"You are an eldest son are you not, Constable?"

"I am, though how you knew it I'll never guess."

"And how old were you when you first went to work earning money for your family."

"Seven Sir," said he.

"And you've younger brothers?"

"Three Mr. Holmes, but what has that to do with the price of ham in Bristol?"

"Only this Constable DeJong, when did your younger brothers begin working for the family."

"Oh I see what you're after now. I guess it would be around twelve Mr. Holmes."

"And such I assure you, is ever the case of it," Holmes remarked confidently. "So when I see a young man of twenty-and-seven riding about the country on a radical new machine which costs more than a common man's home, if he's lucky enough to own one, I know I'm looking at the younger son of a prosperous family. When I see a young man of such wealth working in league with someone like Fitzwilliam DeGreystoke, I know he was attending one of the finest schools in the land and that the two undoubtedly met there and discovered they were cut from the same cloth an of like mind. It only follows that a young man fortunate enough to attend such a school and receive the instruction of such a Professor, must himself be a member of one of the oldest families in the land. So you can see Gentlemen, all of this is quite straightforward."

"And his boxing Holmes?" I reminded.

"The ears Watson."

"The ears?"

"Yes, the ears are one of the most singular sources of information available to us and yet how often are they sadly overlooked. A glance at them may even show the connection between a father and son or an ancestor and his descendants, even where that link is unknown to others. Or, in this case, it may declare a man a seasoned pugilist. Did you not notice the beginning of that condition known as cauliflower ear? It is clear evidence that one is a seasoned boxer?"

Chapter 4 – The King's Castle

On Holmes' advice and Inspector Lestrade's agreement, Inspector Naylor announced that his men would be kept on watch throughout the night and pulled at 6 o'clock in the morning.

"How long do you believe it will be before the

public knows about your lifting of the watch?" Holmes asked the young man.

"Within the hour Mr. Holmes. That part of the great city of Cirencester, which is not asleep, drunk, or unconscious in hospital, will be fully aware within sixty short minutes or less. That is the power of the people hereabouts and the wonder of it can scarcely be described. Had I not seen it at work myself upon numerous occasions you could not induce me to believe it. As it is, however, and me being a Sussex man by birth, I declare myself a converted believer."

"Then I will say my farewell to you and your city Inspector Naylor, and known only to you," Holmes said solemnly, "we will be on tomorrow morning's train."

"I will keep my men away Mr. Holmes, if you really think this will draw them out. It seems like a bold move to return to the scene of their latest escape and I give you long odds Sir, but I know enough to allow myself to be guided by you. I'll wish you good luck."

The following morning Holmes and I made our way to the telegraph office, where he sent a message, and then on to the depot. We sat upon benches along the platform, watching and waiting. Inspector Lestrade and Constable DeJong, now in plain clothes, waited near either end of the depot while a dozen other people milled about or sat waiting patiently with us. I tended to agree with Inspector Naylor's skeptical assessment of Holmes' theory whereby, having escaped capture at the depot only the day before, the criminals once again return to the scene to depart upon the morning express.

For some reason which Holmes had not felt the need to share with me, he believed that Fitzwilliam DeGreystoke would be on the morning train.

"I'll bid you adieu until later Watson," he said, as he rose from the bench. He was in the disguise of an elderly seller of quality hairbrushes, mirrors, and combs, and wore a long, grizzled beard.

Like so many of his disguises I could see virtually nothing of my friend in the man before me. His back was hunched under a worn gray suit of worsted wool, removing a good three inches from Sherlock Holmes' true height. An equally aged black derby topped a mass of curly black hair flecked with gray. As a special touch, the derby's scuff marks had been half-hidden by the careful application of boot black. Unpolished black work boots with thick, worn-down soles, a tired looking cane with dents and scratches along its length, veins traced onto the top of his hands using an artist's paint brush and diluted blue ink, and a leather salesman's bag, finished his look.

"I'll see you inside then," said I.

More people were arriving by the moment and when the train arrived there was a natural rush for the doors. I was in no hurry as I was to take a seat near the door in whichever compartment I found Holmes sitting in. When I arrived at the door and found him seated across from an elegantly attired young gentleman I was surprised. The Gentleman was in as stark a contrast to Holmes' plainness as he could be.

J. B. Varney

His long suit coat and waistcoat were in dove gray, highlighted by a bright, white high-collar, white cravat, white gloves, black pants and patent leather shoes.

I stepped in with a nod to the young gentleman, who looked in my direction, and took my seat next to the door just as I'd been instructed. Holmes kept his pose, hunched over his cane, stared dully out.

I knew our allies, Inspector Lestrade and the stouthearted Constable DeJong, were conducting a thorough search of the train, each from their own end. If they had any luck they would seize the culprits and send a message to us. I, however, only very slowly caught Holmes' subtle signals and by the time I did I could tell he was quite frustrated. Whenever the young man would look out upon the passing scenery, Holmes would point at him with the little finger of his left hand, and this was the signal I failed to comprehend until we were nearly halfway to London.

When I finally did I took a long look at our companion and, very slowly, another person took shape before my eyes. I'd seen the rounded jawline before, somewhere surely, and the ear with the rearward slope, did it display the medical condition known as perichondral hematoma, the cauliflower ear Holmes had spoken of? Indeed it did. The long nose too seemed familiar and then I looked at the eyes, the green eyes! This exquisitely dressed young gentleman with the very long arms and large fists was indeed the working man who'd been on the platform the day before, moving the trunks! That was what Holmes had wanted me to see and understand. I nodded, very much to his satisfaction.

The fearlessness and recklessness of the young man were incredible. Had I just committed the crime of kidnapping I would have been immovable with fear and caution, but not him. Now that I knew who he was I found it difficult to keep from staring. Thus far Holmes' plan had worked beyond all expectation of success, at least in my opinion, for against long odds he had correctly predicted the criminals would take the morning train and at least the young man had done so. Whether DeGreystoke and the Oxford Don were on the train was yet to be seen, but the train was now, for lack of a better term, a fixed abode and with Inspector Lestrade and Constable DeJong on the search it wouldn't be long before we knew.

At that moment a shadow appeared in the doorway and looking up I started involuntarily. There before me stood none other than Fitzwilliam DeGreystoke himself, the wild beard and all.

His head swiveled and turned slowly toward me and it took all my strength to look down. Even then my movement was stiff and unnatural. I was sure the little man had seen through me.

He stared next at Holmes and after several moments he walked silently over and sat next to the young man who, despite not being a large man himself, dwarfed the Professor.

The two men spoke in whispers for a few minutes and while I had only been able to make out a handful of insignificant words, I was sure that

The Oxford Don

Holmes would have learned a great deal.

I fully expected our allies to converge upon the compartment at any second but minutes ticked by as the two kidnappers talked cordially. They covered the prospects of a hot summer, the young man's plans to winter in Italy, and the prospects for Ormonde to take the Triple Crown with a win in the St. Leger Stakes in Doncaster in September.

Then I heard something which I never imagined I would.

"Well Mr. Holmes," the little Professor said, "I suspect you have a plan for all of...this."

The last words were spoken with a flourish of his hand about the compartment.

"And you Sir, Dr. John Watson I presume," he continued, obviously enjoying himself, "what have you to say for your behavior?"

"My behavior?" said I indignantly.

"Now Watson," Holmes nodded, removing his disguise. "Let us not allow Mr. DeGreystoke to gain any satisfaction from the encounter."

"It's Professor DeGreystoke," the young man snapped at Holmes, "and if you don't remember it you can depend upon me taking you to task with more than a little rough instruction," he said, pounding his palm with his fist. "Oh, I know all about you Mr. Holmes. You fancy yourself a pugilist but it's a little thing to dominate the riffraff upon the street, untrained as they are. In me you'll meet a university champion who has both speed and endurance and what, thirty years on you, old man? I assure you I'll enjoy myself."

Holmes, now freed from his grizzled beard and heavy eyebrows and sporting his deerstalker cap again, stared at the young man.

"Mr. John Fothergill," said he, "the younger brother to Joseph, James, and Sarah, of Tarn Hall, Ravenstonedale, Yorkshire. You'd do well not to underestimate the untrained riffraff from the streets for I assure you that untrained is not the same as unschooled. Until you face the folk you disparage, it would be wise to observe the proprieties. By the way, are you not descended from the esteemed Dr. Thomas Fothergill, of Oxford University?"

"Yes, he was the Provost of Queen's College, Oxford," the young man replied proudly, "in the last century, but how come you to know so much of these things? Surely I am not familiar with you."[18]

"We share a common acquaintance," Holmes said cooly.

"Then you are one up on me Sir, for I know of no such man!"

"Oh, I know you do," my friend said with a knowing smile.

"You know nothing Mr. Holmes," DeGreystoke pronounced unequivocally. "You are just a meddler and gossip, a busybody. Oh you've gotten lucky a time or two, to be sure, but I see through your façade. Besides, what would you be without your 'promoter'? That's all the good doctor really is, you know, a mere purveyor of tripe like so many others

---

[18] "The Fothergills of Ravenstonedale: Their Lives and Letters," by Catherine Thornton & Frances McLaughlin, published by William Heinemann, London, page 64.

upon the streets. He earns his money making up the most fantastic stories about you. The fact that the Strand Magazine foists them upon the public as true stories is...absolutely criminal."

"Yes, no doubt," Holmes replied flatly, "save for the scratches upon Mr. Fothergill's neck, just there above the collar on his left side, and the swelling to the left jaw. You will note there is no corresponding fullness upon the right side you see, but I am merely lucky to have observed these things."

Holmes' words had clearly struck a nerve and neither man had a plausible retort.

"What's the matter Mr. Fothergill, did the Oxford Don get the better of our famous Champion Jack! If you can't defend yourself against an aged Professor of Philosophy, a man who stands all of five-feet four-inches in height," Holmes mocked fiercely, "you would certainly be shown up by the riffraff, not to mention yours truly."

The young man nearly came out of his seat but DeGreystoke calmed his friend just enough to keep him down.

"I know we'll be passing a hospital soon Mr. Holmes, but at your age is it really wise to bait a man like Battling Jack Fothergill. He's half your age and has twice the number of fights under his belt, all victories by the bye."

"I think we've talked long enough," Holmes said without raising his voice, "and now I'd like to introduce you to Detective Inspector Lestrade of Scotland Yard!"

The effect of the mention of such a man had an

obviously worrying effect, especially upon Battling Jack Fothergill. As if on cue Lestrade and Constable DeJong appeared at the door.

"Did you find anything?" Holmes asked.

"A locked trunk in the brake van," the Constable said, pulling out his notebook.[19] "It's addressed to the care of F. DeGreystoke, 305 Charing Cross."

"Alright Mr. DeGreystoke," Inspector Lestrade said, without knowing the response Holmes had

---

[19] Brake Van – the term for the crew car at the end of a train in Britain during the Victorian Era. The North American term was caboose until their discontinuation in 1980..

received when he called the man by that title."

The little man's head dropped to his chest and it seemed all the air rushed out of him, leaving him smaller and frailer even than he had already seemed next to the young man. He rose like a prisoner making his last walk to the gallows.

"Watch this one Constable," Lestrade ordered.

"Yes Constable, for he informed us that he was a university boxing champion," Holmes added.

"I don't think I'll have any trouble with that Mr. Holmes, you remember I'm grew up on Redmans Road in Whitechapel and that's an education too."

"I remember very well indeed," Holmes said as he followed me out the door.

Once DeGreystoke got out the door, however, and with the empty passageway before him, he took off like a shot toward the rear of the train. I was almost as shocked that he'd bolted as I was that he could hit such a speed in so short a distance.

"Get him Watson!" Holmes cried as he and Inspector Lestrade raced after me.

We had two corners to navigate and I took the first too quickly, almost dislocating a shoulder in the process. Then we had two dimly lit freight cars crammed full of boxes, barrels, crates, and sundry items to get through. I closed on the man just as he opened the brake van door and our momentum carried us halfway down the car where he collapsed upon the locked trunk, screaming.

I had him in the undignified position of being clapped about at the collar and his left arm and held him down hard upon the trunk.

"Unhand me you lout!" he screamed, as if the volume of his words were a weapon in itself. As I continued to hold him firmly he shook himself the way a little dog might who doesn't like its leash. Then he began to mutter more quietly.

"You barbarians...brutes!" he cried. "Scythians!" he hissed.

"You need to hush yourself," Inspector Lestrade ordered, "you're lucky he hasn't thrown you from the speeding train. Now, where's the key?"

The little man jostled in my grip and looked down like a pouting child who refused to cooperate. Then he reached into a pocket and handed the Inspector a crumpled paper.

As Lestrade turned to the table where a light sat, Holmes stepped forward.

"Come on DeGreystoke," he said, "you can see the game is up. Give us the key."

The man with the wild beard, as Holmes had once described him, looked up and glared at my friend, but produced no key.

"What's this?" the Inspector asked as he looked down at the paper.

Holmes pulled the man's long coat off of him and rifled the pockets until he finally pulled the key out. He tossed the coat to the floor and kicked it aside. I pushed the little man off the trunk and farther down the brake van, where he stood glowering at us, clearly angered at his defeat.

As Holmes undid the clasp and opened the trunk, Inspector Lestrade turned and read out the message on the slip of paper.

The Oxford Don

"King's Castle!" he said, "although what that means is anyone's guess."

"Imbeciles," DeGreystoke said with a satisfied smile. "Fools and their follies go hand in hand."

"There's nothing here but clothing!" Holmes growled as he spun on Fitzwilliam DeGreystoke. Where is he you devil?"

"You must learn your place Holmes. You think you're in control here, but that is only an illusion."

"I, Fitzwilliam DeGreystoke, am in charge and if you ever wish to see your precious Oxford Don alive..."

"What does King's Castle mean?" Lestrade interrupted the man in his obvious moment of glory, infuriating the DeGreystoke even as he turned and handed the paper to Holmes.

"King's Castle is a move in chess," Holmes said quietly. "It enables the king to change places with a rook, thus escaping any foreseeable danger in his former area. It means Professor Findley isn't here. He's been moved somewhere else, isn't that right Professor DeGreystoke?"

The man had retrieved his long coat from the floor where Holmes had cast it, shook it clean, and put it back on. Then he stood in the middle of the brake van staring at us, his hands behind his back, an evil grin upon his twisted face and his eyes full of cruel delight.

"The great Sherlock Holmes," said he derisively, his dignity restored, "finally you've come to realize the true complexity of your situation and the meaning of King's Castle! Now you know how my opponents feel when they meet me in competition Mr. Holmes. It doesn't take them long to realize that I control the board and they can't defeat me, try as they might. King's Castle means I'm in control Inspector Lestrade, not you and certainly not Mr. Sherlock Holmes! Your official position and Mr. Holmes' fleeting fame do nothing for either of you here, no more than Dr. Watson's superior size and strength. No, you may clap me down Doctor, but there is no muscle strong enough to keep me down. Fitzwilliam DeGreystoke is in charge here and you Gentlemen will do exactly as you are told!"

We were all herded back to our compartment, only to discover the acclaimed university boxing champion, Jack Fothergill, stretched out to his full length and unconscious upon the rug.

"He was dead set on pressing me Inspector," the Constable explained, "wanted to get past me he did. Set determined he was too, I tell you."

"What did you do to him, you savage?" the Professor demanded as he looked down upon the young man Holmes had only shortly before called "Champion Jack."

"I clocked 'im a straight right Mr. Holmes," the solidly built Constable admitted, "just the once Sir!"

Holmes gave that barely discernible smile, which was his trademark, but I knew there was a good bit of satisfaction behind it.

J. B. Varney

Chapter 5 – Thespian Talents

Holmes had seemed strangely dejected from the moment he opened the trunk in the brake van and Fitzwilliam DeGreystoke began his monologue. It was as if he had been defeated by the little man and he felt it more than I'd ever witnessed before.

"So this is what it feels like to be truly beaten," he whispered to me in the final seconds before the kidnappers rose to leave the train in Richmond.

Unfortunately for him DeGreystoke overheard his comment and launched into a new tirade.

"Now you know the feeling Mr. Holmes. It is a sensation that will never leave you. Years from now, upon your deathbed even, you'll remember this moment and you'll remember me, the man who defeated the great Sherlock Holmes."

After they left Holmes stood at the window in the passageway and watched them until they were out of sight. As the train began its slow acceleration he spun on the three of us in the compartment, slammed the door shut, and clapped his hands.

"Now Gentlemen," said he happily, "now that we've convinced the braggart that he's beaten us for good, it is time to discuss our next move."

"That was odd Mr. Holmes, that 'King's Castle' thing DeGreystoke came up with."

"It is only natural for a chess champion to think in terms of the game he loves and has mastered, Inspector Lestrade, so to defeat him we must trust to even more effective action."

"So you knew that the Oxford Don wasn't..."

"Professor Findley is currently ensconced at Grimthorpe Manor Watson, either that or I am much mistaken. It is the ancient seat of the DeGreystoke Barons. Fitzwilliam DeGreystoke was never going to risk losing his prize again if he could help it."

"And you knew this all along," I continued my thought, "and you said nothing to me, to us?"

I had long had a complaint against Holmes that he used my services but didn't trust my discretion. This seemed merely a repeat of that old habit.

"It wasn't that I distrusted you Watson, or you for that matter Inspector. Rather it was my goal that you would both react with the natural shock and disappointment that would come from knowing we'd been bested and had failed to recover our Oxford Don, Professor Findley. Had I told you that he wasn't on the train I feared the performance you would give might not be convincing enough to fool our diabolical opponent and I don't need to tell you that it was imperative that we were convincing."

"The little man does strike me as demented in some way," Lestrade confessed.

"There are some trees," Holmes began upon a line of thought I'd heard before, "which grow to a certain height, Inspector, and then suddenly and without the least warning, develop some unsightly eccentricity. You will often see the phenomenon in humans as well. We have just such a case in Professor DeGreystoke I'm afraid."

"I found it more than a little bit...disconcerting," Lestrade admitted honestly. "I'm no fan of the bizarre and macabre, that's for certain. Never have been and I won't spend a shilling on those plays, you know."

"What's been gained though, in all this? That's my thought," the young Constable asked.

"We've been beaten and dismissed," Holmes said. "When Professor DeGreystoke defeats an opponent in his matches that's an end to it. They shake hands and go their separate ways. Both men have agreed subconsciously to the Gentleman's Bargain even if they never say it aloud. The winner will not belittle the loser and the latter will not complain of any kind of unfair advantage to his foe. They will go their separate ways and if one or the other wishes for a rematch, even that has a proper process which must be observed upon all occasions. Braggadocio and poor sportsmanship are not the commodities of either a gentleman or a champion chessman."

"He expects we'll quit the field?" I said in shock.

"He believes we've been bested. He believes his stratagem has stymied us and we simply have no idea where to turn next."

"But it hasn't stymied us, has it Mr. Holmes?"

"No it hasn't Constable DeJong and here I will tell you a story which may yet have exercise some bearing upon the outcome of the case of the Oxford Don. Although the event was of no significance to DeGreystoke then and therefore made little enough an impression on his mind, we met once before in passing at Christ Church College Oxford. I was around your age then Constable and we were both the guests of Professor Findley, who even in his days as a single man stocked his pantry with many an uncommon delicacy. So much so in fact that an invitation to dine there was seen as godsend by most."

"Well, I listened to the men's conversation with great attention and after an uncommonly fine meal I was challenged to a best-of-three set by Professor DeGreystoke. He imagined it would be a short run thing no doubt and after the first game, an abysmal defeat for me, he had good reason for his view. I took the second game however and it came as very much a shock to both DeGreystoke and Findley. The former simply didn't lose chess games, the total number of such things being counted upon but one hand I believe, even now. I know had certainly never lost to a student just beginning his first term."

Holmes had made his point, that he'd once defeated the great chessman, and as was his way he simply left the story unfinished. My friend had the confounding tendency to make no accounting for human curiosity and it was only when the Constable asked about the third game that Holmes continued.

"Oh, well, the game went three hours and we called a stalemate past midnight."

"That is incredible Mr. Holmes," the Inspector remarked, "but you don't believe the man recalls you, either by face or name?"

"A shadowy image in a misty past, Inspector," Holmes said, "nothing more."

"Surely, with his memory..." I began.

"Great men rarely focus upon their defeats

Watson. If they did, Napoleon would never have ventured into Russia. This principle is especially true where their most embarrassing reverses are concerned. I can assure you that DeGreystoke very quickly relegated that evening to the most upsetting of losses and it was very soon swept under the proverbial carpet. Furthermore I saw no recognition at the sight of my face nor did he make any reference to my name, beyond the fact that I had gained a kind of fame, even if fleeting, mainly from the mostly fictional stories of the good Doctor. No, he does not place me as the young man who played him to a draw on that bygone evening in Professor Findley's salon, and it is my hope to use that against him."

"I beg your pardon Mr. Holmes, but I don't see how a few chess games some twenty-odd years ago can have the slightest bearing upon the situation we now find ourselves in."

"Have you ever noticed that the personalities of some couples fit together to a remarkable degree and from the very outset of their relationship?" Holmes asked mysteriously.

"I suppose I have," Inspector Lestrade admitted, "although I'd say that such a thing is a rarity."

"Indeed," Holmes said dismissively, "a rarity, we can even call it one-in-a-hundred thousand if you like, but you have seen it?"

"Yes, I said I suppose I have."

"Now," said he with a flourish, "I've recognized a similar principle at work between adversaries, although it is anything but a harmonious joining together. Rather, I propose that between the most resolute competitors or opponents, you will upon occasion find one who is especially gifted with an ability to see into the weaknesses of the other. Where most people will be all but blind to those weaknesses or frailties, this one person will be blessed to a high degree with the insight. Wellington possessed this in regard to Napoleon. Alexander too, made supreme use of it in his overthrow of Darius and the Persians."

"And you propose that you have such a...vision in regard to Professor DeGreystoke?" I asked.

"I would love to say that my superior intellect, even in my relative youth, was sufficient to best one of England's greatest chess champions in one game and stalemate him in another, thus ending the series in a draw, but I cannot. You may recall that DeGreystoke has defeated the German Champion, Anderssen by name, and the Austrian Champion, Steinitz, not to mention Von Soltesz, whom we've already discussed Watson."

"Yes," said I, "the Hungarian master and all truly impressive as well, but I'm afraid I still don't see the point."

"He defeats three of the world's greatest chess players Watson, probably of all time, then goes on to lose to an unseasoned student and is forced, quite against his every effort I might add, to accept a draw. Do you know what the mathematical odds of such an event occurring are, even once in a lifetime, even in a population group as large as our own."

"It does seem unlikely now that you put it like

that," I confessed.

"Unlikely! It's absolutely inconceivable."

"But this, you say Mr. Holmes, is just what proves that you have some kind of insight into DeGreystoke's weaknesses?"

"Can you think of any other solution, Inspector? One which meets all the facts."

Holmes possessed a peculiarly introspective way which was, I'd found, a leading characteristic of his.

All the subjects which captivated him were eventually and inevitably considered in the deepest fashion possible. His notion that a thing was not known until all of that thing was known completely, reflected his view. His penchant for the writing of monographs, which I'd seen were overseen in the driest and most technical manner possible, also echoed this approach. He had dubbed his theory regarding adversaries 'The Devil's Paradox' and had declared several times that he would put it into monograph form.

"I can," Constable DeJong volunteered, "I'd say that you're brilliant Mr. Holmes and more brilliant than this other fellow, DeGreystoke. That fits all the facts, don't it?"

"Thank you Constable," Holmes said, clearly amused by the young man's exclamation, "it is certainly the simplest solution, I'll give you that."

"So to return to the earlier point Holmes, as you have this special insight into our opponent and we aren't stalemated by his move, where do we turn next? What are we to do?"

"You know my methods. What can you deduce

from the man you've encountered?"

"Come now Holmes," I insisted. "What can I gather from the little I've seen of DeGreystoke?"

"As I've said before my dear Watson, it isn't the quantity of evidence, which is the most important thing, but rather the quality of the information from which one can draw."

I sat back and put my chin in my hand. We still had some time before we reached Waterloo Station but I felt very much up against it. After a few minutes I threw my hands up.

"I can make nothing of it," said I.

"And yet you see everything I see," Holmes insisted. "Let us reason from what we've witnessed and see where that leads us."

"Pray do so Mr. Holmes for we are nearly to our destination and as matters stand we shall return to the Yard with empty hands.

"The first item of importance which we know is that DeGreystoke is a man of means and has long been used to that circle of society for whom the doors are, as they say, ever open."

"True enough, but whether that has any bearing upon the case is yet to be seen Mr. Holmes."

"Surely Inspector, you will not deny that a man raised with country homes and ancient family castles and estates at his disposal possesses options which the dweller of a Whitechapel tenement does not."

"No," Lestrade agreed, "as far as that goes I would not deny it."

"Nor could you argue that a man raised in such an environment would not have developed a mind which recognizes far fewer limitations than his Whitechapel counterpart."

"I suppose that would be plausible, in so far as it went."

"What do you mean, 'so far as it went,' for the mind makes the man more so than any other single factor, does it not? And the man who honestly believes he can solve any problem he faces will think much differently than the man who is unsure where the next month's rent may be coming from."

"You have me there Mr. Holmes if that was your goal, for no one will argue that the wealthy look at the world very differently than the poor."

"My point is, Inspector, that DeGreystoke will not only make use of his resources in seeing this crime to its conclusion, but also that he would have considered them throughout his planning. It has become increasingly clear that the goal of the famed chess master is to dispose of his enemy and never answer for the crime. Not only this, but he means to carry it out in such a way that his reputation is never stained even by the rumors of such a crime."

"I'm afraid he will find the law stands in his way," Lestrade vowed.

"He does not see the law as an insurmountable obstacle," Holmes replied, "by which I deduce that this is not DeGreystoke's first venture into the world of base criminality."

This last was a mysterious comment, pointing as it did to some as yet unknown crime or crimes about which we knew nothing.

"It is suggestive though," Holmes said.

"So the first point was that he is a man of means and will use his fortune and properties to carry out this kidnapping," the Inspector remarked, "and the second point Mr. Holmes?"

"The second, yes. That is...more complex. As to that I believe there is a residual vulnerability in our opponent which we can use to predict his actions, at least to some degree. I mentioned that among certain men their most upsetting failures and defeats will be swept under the carpet. However, the clearing of the memory is one thing while the cleansing of the subconscious is quite another. On the one level he can easily dismiss that evening in Professor Findley's salon, but upon the deeper level he continues to wrestle with the fear of unexpected defeat and the sense of helplessness he felt at not being able to salvage a victory out of that moment and that despite so completely overmatching his opponent. The result of that can be seen in the extra effort he has put into insulating himself from the possibility of a repeat of that event. He may not even be aware of what he is doing or why?"

"He would not put his king, Professor Findley, in a position where he could be recaptured," I said.

"Indeed Watson and we found the trunk filled with what? With clothes and not with the kidnapped man. That confirmed everything for us. The safest and therefore most likely place for his incarceration, as I said, is at Grimthorpe itself. He would not allow himself to be defeated and his method, quite brilliant as it also formed an insurance plan, was to remove his king from the board altogether."

The Oxford Don

"Not very sporting, that," Lestrade noted.

"No, you're quite right there Inspector," Holmes agreed, "but then one need not look twice upon Mr. DeGreystoke to note that he very likely never ran and bled upon the playing fields of Eton!"[20]

Holmes' point was that Fitzwilliam DeGreystoke had never had to learn the importance of playing by the rules on the playing fields because he repudiated the physical so thoroughly that he would have avoided it at all costs. As Dean Liddell had said, "I'm afraid that in the rarified world of academia Dr. Watson, we find it very easy to inflate the value of the mind over the merely physical. Mankind's brute nature is seen as set against our higher self."

"Before we were ready to go there, however, we first had to put on our act to convince Professor DeGreystoke that we'd been defeated and were no longer either in play or in possession of any idea where to look."

"And you think we convinced him?" I asked.

"You all did superbly," Holmes said.

"Probably because we really thought we'd find the poor victim there," Inspector Lestrade said, his ashen complexion even paler than usual. "So now we need to go to Grimthorpe Manor?"

"Yes, while DeGreystoke believes we are bound for 305 Charing Cross Road, London, the address upon the trunk in the brake van and obviously a

---

[20] "The battle of Waterloo was won on the playing fields of Eton," the Duke of Wellington. The actual quote was spoken while watching a sporting event at Eton. "The battle of Waterloo was won here." Source: George W. Stimpson, author.

ruse, we must look elsewhere. The game is afoot Gentlemen," he said with that same look of joy which always accompanied those four words, "The game is afoot."

Holmes and Lestrade both sent messages off from the station, then we took the Maidstone train to the village of Charing Heath. The bustling village was set amid the broad, tranquil vale of the Medway and the Great Stour. As our destination was up on the high plateau of the Kent Downs to the east, we set about hiring a cart and driver and were soon off upon the winding ascent up the Hart Hill Road which led us to our destination, the village of Stalisfield Green. We took rooms in the Plough Inn around noon.

Had it been up to Holmes we would have been off immediately, scouting about the countryside for Grimthorpe Manor and the best approach to make in the night. With the two policemen along, however, I had just the allies I needed to push for a good English lunch before beginning our adventure. While we ate at the Plough, Holmes sipped his coffee and looked about the Inn.

"I say, Innkeeper," said he as he approached the bar, "we are historians out for the day in search for an historic castle in these parts."

"You must be speaking of Grimthorpe Manor, Sir," the publican replied.

"Indeed, that is the very place," said Holmes warmly, "Is it a long walk or must we hire a cart?"

"It is a good mile across the fields but a wet spring makes it too much for travel. It's half again as much by road, but the folk up there are..."

The man paused uncomfortably and jostled with some dishes during which time Holmes seemed to comprehend his meaning.

"The folk up there are a private lot are they?"

"Aye, that's one way o' puttin' it," said he in strong agreement, "but they're good customers and I'd not want to lose their trade for anything."

"Well, we'll try to be...circumspect," Holmes said mysteriously.

"This is their chief just here," the innkeeper said, nodding out the window and into the road where a dashing figure in a broad-brimmed straw hat and long black coat alighted gracefully from a cart.

"Their chief?" Holmes asked, clearly surprised, for the man could not have looked more unlike the diminutive Fitzwilliam DeGreystoke. "Are not the DeGreystoke's still lords of Grimthorpe?"

"Oh, they are Sir, but Mr. George Venner there, he's a cousin through the distaff line.[21] He manages the place."

"And what of Fitzwilliam DeGreystoke?"

"Aye, he's the undisputed owner, to be sure," the man said, "after those untimely deaths...everything is his now. There's no disputing that, only he isn't round much and everyone knows that Mr. Venner is the one in charge over there."

"A sizeable group then?" Holmes asked.

---

[21] A distaff is a stick used in the hand-spinning process. As spinning was seen as a task within the woman's sphere, the term became applied to the mother's ancestral line. The "distaff side" or the "distaff line" were common terms in the Victorian Age.

Just then Mr. George Venner entered, hailed the publican with a comfortable wave of the hand, and pointed to a corner table with a view of the road.

"Excuse me Sir," the Innkeeper said, leaving Holmes and taking a cup of coffee to his newest customer.

Holmes returned to our table without drawing attention to himself by staring, but I could see the tension upon his face.

The new arrival paid us little enough attention and was joined shortly by another gentleman of the same confident stamp and what I recognized as a military air.

"Thomas," said the first, joyously, "I wondered I'd ever see you again."

"Indeed, that last business put us in a tight spot Venner."

"Well, one hardly imagines he will ever be in the center of such fierce fighting," Venner said.

"I could live the rest of my life and never wish to encounter another ordeal like we saw at Amoaful."[22]

"Queen and Country!" said Mr. George Venner, only half joking.

"Here, here!" said the other, lifting a freshly deliver cup in toast. "So what's this business you wrote about?"

"It's a business that will put some coin in your pocket old son and if you're still in the same boat as me, that's a welcome thing."

"It's true enough that the civilian world has been

---

[22] The Battle of Amoaful, fought early in 1874, was the decisive battle of the Third Anglo-Ashanti War.

less than generous with your old friend, Cuthbert Creighton," the second man laughed.

"I'll say more on that topic once we're back to the castle."

"The castle? So you weren't joking? I wondered about that."

"No, I look after a regular medieval pile," Mr. George Venner acknowledged. "It's like something out of one of those horrid 'Penny Dreadfuls,' you know the stuff."

"You mean like that gothic 'Varney the Vampire' story they keep grinding out."[23]

"You'll see," Venner said, as their conversation turned to more mundane subjects and we finished our lunch.

Holmes' gave a knowing nod to our host and placed a sovereign upon the table.

"Historians?" Mr. Holmes, Inspector Lestrade asked curiously once we were outside.

"Better that than our exposure Inspector, for in such an empty district the sudden appearance of four such characters can only lead to speculation among the locals."

"So it wouldn't have been long before Mr. George Venner learned about our presence even if he hadn't seen us himself," I acknowledged.

"Did I gather those two were Army men, Dr. Watson?" Lestrade asked.

"Yes," I replied, "they had the look about them

---

[23] Varney the Vampire – a gothic horror story series by James Malcolm Rymer and Thomas Peckett Prest, printed in the era in weekly pamphlets known as 'penny dreadfuls'.

from the start and then, by their conversation, they confirmed it. They served in the Third Ashanti Expedition."

"That was what, '78?" he speculated.

"'73 and '74 mainly."

"The first was an officer of one of your cavalry regiments Watson," said Holmes in that manner which attached all military matters to me, "and the other was with the royal artillery."

"Surely there is no way for anyone to know such things Mr. Holmes, as the men said nothing with regard to their units," Lestrade quipped.

"You are correct in the latter statement, that they shared nothing that might reveal their unit or units, however, in your supposition that there was no way to know such things, I assure you that you are quite mistaken."

"But surely the one implies the other," I said.

"If such a principle is in force Watson, then can you not see that it would also apply to your own initial conclusion about the men, that they were Army men...because they 'had the look about them.'"

This puzzling twist undid me, for if I were able to deduce what I had, then most certainly Sherlock Holmes would've been able to deduce much more.

"How was it done then Mr. Holmes," Constable DeJong asked, earnestly.

We had walked up the road some way by now, to the location of a livery, and took a cart and horse for the remainder of the day. Ostensibly our goal was to inspecting the vicinity around the village but

Holmes' true purpose was to view Grimthorpe Manor and its surrounding park.

"First of all," Holmes answered, "you will find that the way a man walks is a most suggestive reflection of his life. It speaks volumes to his formative experiences and, sometimes, even his vocation. Furthermore it may be had simply enough through observation and deduction. If you have ever had the chance to watch a man walk who has served in the infantry for example, you will witness one of the greatest cases for observation. His step is sure and evenly paced, rapid without appearing at all hurried, and always in a straight line. By contrast it might be easily judged that a man who goes in an irregular line of travel never served a day in one of our infantry units."

"Unless he'd been at his favorite tipple," the Inspector forwarded glibly.[24]

"There is that" Holmes replied, "although that would lead one to make other deductions." Then he continued. "A cavalryman has had to focus upon other things, namely the art of moving in harmony with an animal of two-thousand pounds or better. The singularities of this are as pronounced as that attached to the infantry or even more so. Similar to the relationship of a man long accustomed to sailing upon the sea, the cavalryman, while he becomes accustomed to and skilled in the art of riding, by the same degree becomes less sure upon terra firma. As a result he will stride the earth with a somewhat

---

[24] Tipple – referring to alcoholic beverages, to drink alcohol.

wider stance than the infantryman. It is a gait which of necessity will present the appearance of a slight swaying from side to side. While this may be so slight as to be imperceptible in itself Constable, I assure you that were you to put the infantryman and the cavalryman side-by-side and commanded them to walk, the difference would be glaringly clear to you. Such is the power of our military's training even in the years after our men leave the services."

"It's all so incredible Mr. Holmes," the young man exclaimed, sincerely.

"Not at all," Holmes remonstrated, "it is all quite elementary Constable."

"You spoke just now Mr. Holmes of observation and deduction," Lestrade responded, "but I noticed that you said nothing as to your deduction that the second man, Mr. Cuthbert Creighton, was lately of the artillery or about how you knew that Venner was an officer."

"It is simplicity itself, Inspector," Holmes said, shaking his head in wonder at Lestrade, "and so much dependent upon observation as to require no deduction at all. It might even serve to define the limits between the two. First, we have the evidence of the Innkeeper, which by itself might prove nothing, but which, when combined with the comments which come later from the two men, becomes powerfully indicative."

"You'll have to make matters a little clearer for me Mr. Holmes, if I'm to follow, for I am but a humble Detective Inspector at Scotland Yard."

"Well then, you heard the same comment I did, that 'everyone knows that Mr. Venner is the one in charge here.' And as I said, taken alone this might be of little value in our determinations, but this was followed in short order by Mr. Cuthbert Creighton's statement about some business putting them both in what he called, "a tight spot," and one he wished never to repeat. This seemed clear enough, but Mr. George Venner's response, 'Queen and Country,' removed all doubt that they were speaking of some military 'business.' Creighton's passing reference to Amoaful, which you may recall from the papers at the time was the key battle ending the hostilities, removed all doubt."

"I can see that now," Lestrade said, as our horse turned down an east running road and we began passing fields, woods, old ruins, and farms in varying degrees of upkeep, "but none of what you've said explains either point, the officer or the artillery."

"The first point I'm attempting to prove is that both men definitely served in the military and the 'business' they were referring to was a war. You may recall Mr. Creighton saying that the civilian world had been less than generous with him. The second is the observation that Mr. Creighton is quite deaf in his right ear."

"Deaf in his right ear?" said I.

"Quite correct Watson."

"But I confess that I don't see how you arrived at this."

"When he rejoined his friend he kept his head turned markedly to his own right side, with his left

The Oxford Don

ear facing the sound coming from his companion. Each time Mr. George Venner spoke Creighton turned his left ear toward him. It was a natural movement, by which I knew that the loss was one of several years at least, and not so obvious a gesture that it would raise a general attention. By the same token, however, it was consistent enough that a keen observer couldn't have missed it."

"Remarkable," I replied.

"As to Mr. George Venner's being an officer, I'm afraid I took some liberty there. The only evidence I had upon which to base that deduction were the Innkeeper's words, as I said, that everyone in these parts knew that Mr. Venner was 'the one in charge here.' To this I added Venner's own behavior when he entered the public house and made his order with nothing more the wave of his hand. This was the mark of a man well used to having authority and exercising his power freely."

"You are a blooming wizard Mr. Holmes!" the young constable exclaimed.

Holmes waved away the compliment though his smile showed it had pleased him.

"To go back to the morning express for a moment Holmes," said I, "how was it you came to know the background of Battling Jack Fothergill so thoroughly upon the train, for I'd swear you didn't know that much before?"

"Our first stop was to the telegraph office where you knew I sent a message, but there was also a reply waiting for me on just that subject Watson. I had wired a description of the young man to a Fellow who works with DeGreystoke at his new school. He recognized Jack Fothergill immediately and, understanding that he was helping on an important case, happily filled me in upon the particulars."

"And now Mr. Holmes?" Lestrade asked.

Our little horse turned down a long, wooded lane and Holmes gestured about.

"Take it all in Gentlemen, every path, for we are anything but historians upon holiday."

Chapter 6 – The Golden Pince-Nez

We continued our explorations in the cart far into the evening when darkness had begun to cast its black hue all about the country. Yet, while our course seemed random enough to anyone caring to watch, our path took us past Grimthorpe Manor three times. It was during the last passage that Holmes came up the narrow lane alone. I'd been left at one location to wait for his return on foot and our two companions were left at another location.

The moon was full and would have been surprisingly bright had it not been for the clouds which continued to roll by in front of it.

"Watson?" came the hoarse whisper from the road a half hour later.

"Here," I replied.

"I say, have you solved the case of the Oxford Don yet, or what?" he whispered jokingly.

"Yes," I snapped, "single-handedly and in a black copse of Yew trees at that, but I would have preferred it if we could have done this before Creighton, that second stalwart veteran, had arrived upon the scene."

"Never fear," he said near my ear. "Two men united after a long separation and discussing old days of danger and excitement, present us with less than half a man by way of diligent observance."

"What a strange compensation, that the arrival of Mr. Cuthbert Creighton might actually prove an advantage to our cause?" I said, surprised.

"In this instance I believe it will, Watson. This is to say nothing of the hounds and the other men however, for none of them will likely be less vigilant because of the arrival of a second soldier."

"Well, I suppose that would be too much to hope for."

"One can always hope," he said, distractedly, "but have you heard anything of our Police chaps?"

"I believe I heard their passage to the west twenty minutes ago, some snapping branches, but nothing more."

"Then they have a good head start on us."

"It might have been some of the red deer they keep in the estate though."

"The passage of one of the fleet-footed beasts would have sounded quite different from the flat-footed variety which you and I have loosed upon the grounds, I'm sure Watson."

We began our passage in through the verge at the point where we had noticed a trail during our daylight tour of the area. In the darkness, however, it was a true challenge and at one point I nearly despaired of success.

"We sound like a herd of elephants, Holmes," I whispered as quietly as possible.

"It does seem counterproductive," he admitted, still in the excellent spirits which often overtook him during the hunt. "Once over the wall though, I've been counting the paces. We should reach the meadow behind the Manor in but a few more minutes. Matters will proceed more rapidly after that."

I wanted to believe him but my mood was not as cheerful nor my expectations quite as hopeful as my friend's. Still, in only a couple minutes the light brightened around us markedly and soon we found ourselves looking over the very meadow Holmes had predicted.

"Get down," he hissed as he pulled my sleeve and nearly jerked me off my feet.

In the distance, upon the lawns of Grimthorpe Manor itself, a pack of hounds came sweeping around the edifice at full tear, their baying carrying across the meadow like some primeval warning.

"Shouldn't we run?"

"Run where Watson? Look at them? Are they not incredible animals?"

"Incredible," I repeated, stunned, for the pack presented us with a bloodcurdling sight.

"They'd have us in a minute if they wanted us," said he, "fortunately for us Watson, we're quite safe from the pack, being downwind from them. The darkness renders their keen sight negligible and it is impossible for them to get our scent when the wind is in our face. In any case running in the dark this far from the wall, we'd be taken before we could get started. The only safety from them tonight is to be found in the trees, so while we skirt the meadow we'll stay close to the oak and maple, all around to the lawns."

"You mean to continue, even with the..."

"Shhh!" said he, suddenly, "did that not sound like a man's scream?"

"Are you...quite serious?" I asked, now more than a little troubled. "The only other men out here are Lestrade and the Constable!"

"Precisely!" said he. "Come Watson, let us take advantage of their pursuit."

With that Holmes went into a sprint through the tall grass which I could never match and while he was roaming to-and-fro about the lawn in the nearly complete darkness, I was still in the meadow following up.

He'd vanished around the corner of a fortified wall which I knew to be the barbican, with two small towers looming over the closed gate to an enclosed square.

As I came around, full of apprehension, I found my friend laid out prone upon the ground.

"Are you alright Holmes?" I barely whispered. "Have you been shot or what?"

"Keep watch Watson," he replied, "and if we must escape it's through the verge, just there," he pointed, and into a tree!"

He was transported into that realm of danger and risk which terrified me, but simultaneously met some deep need within him. I watched and listened with every bit of my power. I heard no baying, which I took to be a bad sign, for I believed the pack of mastiffs was on its return leg and would come racing around the old castle Manor which had set upon that spot since the twelve-hundreds at any moment. I saw no lights at all in the vast black building which loomed above us and only the moonlight, shifting as it was between the banks of clouds, provided any relief from the darkness.

Then I heard the call of a man's voice in the distance. It was George Venner or I was much mistaken and he was getting closer.

"Come Holmes, it's too late," I called, as I sprinted for the verge of thick hedge between the cultivated lawn inside and the wild woods beyond. If I thought I'd run through, as Holmes had said, I was sadly mistaken and was brought to a painful stop by thick, mature branches, interwoven no doubt over a century. I ended by jumping up and rolling over the painful top of the hedge.

I got into the woods and found Holmes right behind me. He stopped me at the base of a good climbing oak and we listened.

"You surprise me Watson," said he in a low voice, "the way you hurdled that hedge I thought you a college sprinter out for a moonlit run."

"Indeed," I said, "with a pack of mastiffs and George Venner upon my heels. Now let us be gone from this place."

Even as I finished this sentence the voices of men upon the lawn came to us.

"Did you see anything?" the one asked.

"Nothing, but a look in the daylight would be good, just to confirm."

"It's likely those deer my cousin insists we keep; I know its them the dogs go chasing. Half the time I can't get a solid night's sleep because of them."

"That won't do!" the other man said, "I need my sleep or I can't function."

"I'll put them in the kennel as soon as they get back," the first man replied. "I'll keep them in the next few days just so we have some peace."

"Why does your cousin want to keep the deer?"

The men walked on and their voices died out around the barbican.

"Did you hear that Watson? Tomorrow night we'll have clear sailing."

"Yes, thanks to the red deer."

We spent an uncomfortable hour up the oak tree until we heard the kennel doors slamming shut and knew the hounds were away. Then we cautiously climbed down and Holmes returned to his searching of the lawn. I had no clue what he hoped to find but the odds of him doing so were so low in that darkness that I feared we'd wasted a good night's sleep for nothing.

It was half-past four in the morning when we returned to the yard of the Plough and found Inspector Lestrade and Constable DeJong sitting outside the public house in the bright moonlight, the clouds having long since passed on.

As we approached Lestrade rose with a groan of pain and the Constable explained that one of the hounds had taken a bite of his boss as they scaled the wall to get away.

"I thought that pack of devils had me for sure," Lestrade moaned bitterly. "What we were doing out there anyway, I can't say."

"There were difficulties of course," Holmes replied. "There are always complications, but you may be certain our joint expedition of this dark night was well worth it."

By this time, and to Inspector Lestrade's complete consternation, Holmes had found an extra key beneath a flowerpot at the front door and quietly let us all in.

"Shoes off," said he, as we entered, and one-by-one, like criminals, we made our way in a line across the pub and up the stairs.

"Stay to the left and you'll avoid the squeaks, then go into Watson's room at the front, where no one will hear us speaking."

"Why did you say tonight was well worth it?" I asked when we'd closed the door and turned up a lamp.

"Because Watson, I found these."

With that Sherlock Holmes pulled something from his pocket and laid a pair of Belgian-made golden pince-nez eyeglasses down upon the desk in front of all our shocked faces.

"His?" I asked.

"Definitely!"

"How can you be so self-assured Mr. Holmes?" Lestrade asked. "After all, England is a big country and who's to say those glasses haven't been lost in the grounds of Grimthorpe Manor for years?"

"For one," Holmes said, "the condition of the glasses is pristine proving they could not have weathered more than a day in that place. For another, of all the items I might have found, I find a pair of Belgian-made golden pince-nez eyeglasses which match Professor Findley's exactly? And lastly, we find them in the grounds of a twelfth century castle now owned by none other than the very man I identified as the Professor's kidnapper, Fitzwilliam DeGreystoke. At what point, Inspector, will you admit what the plain facts tell you?"

Inspector Gerard Lestrade had long considered my friend too cocksure of himself and too quick to make judgments, however, Holmes had proven himself every time.

"So you believe that your Professor was brought to Grimthorpe Manor and was walked about the grounds where his glasses subsequently fell off, only to be found later by you, in the grass in the middle of a black night?"

"No," Holmes replied calmly, "I believe that he was brought to Grimthorpe Manor and placed in a room or cage in the basement of the old castle. Someplace with but one tiny window for air, built in the time when a deep moat encompassed the place in ancient times. He then managed to open the window or remove a pane without be found out, then at his first opportunity he threw his pince-nez out upon the grounds where I subsequently found them, in the dark of night!"

"For what purpose Mr. Holmes?"

"Obviously for the purpose of me finding them and thereby confirming his presence within, Inspector."

"You've done it again Mr. Holmes!" Constable DeJong mumbled excitedly. "I don't know how, but you've done it again. The worst thing about it, Sir, is that I won't be able to tell the fellows, as none of them would ever believe such a thing was even possible."

"No doubt they would label you a liar or, at best, an exaggerator," I commiserated.

I knew of what I spoke for there had always been a small but vocal portion among my readership who never ceased declaring my stories too fabulous and far-fetched to be true. Mr. Fitzwilliam DeGreystoke himself had made such a speech upon the train, declaring my stories to be purely fictional accounts meant to boost my friend up and into a position of undeserved fame.

"You must console yourself, Constable, knowing that the tellers of truth are always labeled thus. It is always the boldest liars who are believed most quickly and easily. You may take Sherlock Holmes' word for it. It is perhaps best, however, that in this particular case the less the fellows back at the Yard heard, the better."

"So you think Professor Findley is imprisoned somewhere deep in Grimthorpe Manor?" Lestrade asked.

"No," Holmes answered, "I know that Professor Findley is imprisoned in the dungeons there."

"You may not know this Mr. Holmes, but I have often complained to my superiors that despite your many gifts, which I have never denied mind you, that you are too certain of yourself and jump to the wildest conclusions without adequate consideration. Would you not agree that in this case my words have been proven true?"

"You surprise me Inspector," said my friend, "Look at it in this way if you will. Malcolm Findley disappears. The only person he can communicate

The Oxford Don

with is in London, so he leaves the only clue he can in a half-finished sentence on his chalk board. I am visited by the college authorities and take on the search for my old mentor, their leading Oxford Don, even though they have already given the kidnapper a forty-eight-hour advance. Despite the mystery I track him from Christ Church College, Oxford, to Dryman House near Cirencester, and then on to Grimthorpe Manor in Kent, and still I find myself doubted by you. I then enter the grounds of the old Manor during the only time I can, in the dark of night, and I find the very man's pince-nez in the grass, and still you fall back upon your stale criticisms. I then crawl to the window in question and tap out a message using the New International Morse Code.[25] My message is simple, 'who are you?' to which I received the response, 'M. Findley,' and with that, my dear Inspector, I very much hope we can finally put your...concerns regarding Mr. Sherlock Holmes to a final and permanent...rest. What do you say to that?"

I had seen my friend in a thousand different situations, many of them ranking as the most amazing kind, and never could I remember being so struck by his genius. From the look upon the young Constable's face I could see that I was not alone in my opinion.

"I very much fear, Mr. Holmes, that I have for too long allowed my petty jealousies of you to

---

[25] Morse Code was introduced in 1844. A new, simplified version of the code, the result of collaboration, came in 1865. It was called "The International Morse Code."

influence my thinking," Lestrade said, shocking all of us with his honest confession. "My superiors have gladly entertained any and all of my complaints against you, happy no doubt with anything that might diminish your standing."

With this Lestrade stood up and straightened himself.

"You have my sincere apologies Sir," said he, earnestly extending his hand.

After the two men had settled their longstanding contretemps, Lestrade spoke again.

"I promise you Mr. Holmes, that we will gather a force together and retrieve Professor Findley even if we must storm the place."

"I appreciate your zeal Inspector, but that will never do. DeGreystoke made it clear that he will kill our man before he allows us to get to him. He will have made that as clear to Mr. George Venner as he did his wishes that the red deer upon his estate are left in peace."

"And you have no doubt in regard to Venner's obedience?" the Inspector asked.

"Not in the least I'm afraid to say."

"Then what do you propose?"

"I propose that the good Doctor sees to your leg and then you retire to your bed. We will gather again tomorrow, not earlier than lunch for you need your rest, and we will discuss our plan then. Until then I wish you Gentlemen a good rest."

Just as Holmes had said, we gathered the next day for lunch in the busy pub and ate quietly. It was clear to me that Inspector Lestrade was suffering from his wound, a deep bite in the thickest part of his calf.

"Those hounds are terrible things," said he, to my comment about his wound. "I'm afraid I'll be no good to you tonight Mr. Holmes."

I was pleased to hear him say it for it was also my professional opinion as well.

"You must leave that to us," Holmes replied, "knowing you will be well represented by Constable DeJong."

"Indeed, I have no doubt that he shall be a credit and do us proud."

Later in Holmes room I asked what had been on my mind since I'd heard it.

"How did you know there would be something to find upon the grounds of Grimthorpe?"

"I was wondering the same thing Mr. Holmes," the Constable added.

"It was a deduction based upon what I know of the mind of Professor Malcolm Findley."

"But how would he have known you'd even be there, at Grimthorpe?" Lestrade asked.

"Yes," Holmes said, with a smile, "that too was a deduction. In this case however, it was Professor Findley who believed I'd be upon the scene shortly. His deductions were based upon what he knew of my mind."

"But I thought they were keeping him drugged Mr. Holmes?" Constable DeJong remarked.

"And no doubt they believe they are for it is certainly their intention. The truth is that the only way to achieve such a goal with such a man as

Malcolm Findley is to continually inject him with the suitable drugs. As such a thing is impractical, for several reasons, they would have taken to supplying him the drug in his food. Professor Findley would eat only enough to keep himself functioning and then he would have eaten that portion of each meal least likely to be effected by the sedative, the underside of a portion of meat and so forth. Only by mixing the drug thoroughly through other food items would they be able to insure he would get the dosage, but by minimizing his intake he could largely counter their efforts."

"How would he deal with the remaining food, for surely they would see he was barely eating?" I asked.

"He would hide it wherever he could and horde as much of it as possible."

"To what purpose Mr. Holmes?" the Inspector asked, a new respect clear in his voice.

"He will use it this afternoon," Holmes replied, "upon George Venner's favorite hound, Goliath."

These words astounded all of us as the revealed Holmes much deeper knowledge of conditions inside Grimthorpe Manor.

"Your Morse Code," I cried. "You learned far more than you told us?"

"Yes," Holmes admitted, "the animal is massive and the food Professor Findley has been able to hoard has been limited. It should at least have some beneficial effect upon the animal, at least in as far as we're concerned. Even if it only slows him that will be something."

"But I thought they were keeping the hounds in Mr. Holmes?" the Constable asked.

"Indeed, but Goliath is a different case. He generally goes where George Venner goes, although he is put out to roam freely at certain times."

"But you still plan to strike tonight?"

"I do Inspector. It will be tonight or else we may be too late to help. I'm afraid I didn't tell you about two people I had planted on the morning express. When DeGreystoke and Fothergill departed the train in Richmond they were followed."

"Billy Wiggins," I said, knowing he was one of Holmes' most trusted boys in the Irregulars.

"People rarely notice the young or the elderly," Holmes replied. "They've been under observation since and from this telegram, which I received this morning, it appears they've made plans to travel to Grimthorpe tomorrow."

"Then it's now or never," I declared.

"It does seem that our drama draws to a close. It is more complex than you may suspect, however, for while we see to the rescue of Professor Findley we must not lose sight of the capture of Fitzwilliam DeGreystoke and his gang. If we cannot scoop them up in a net at the same time they'll no doubt go to ground and escape justice indefinitely."

"Just how dangerous is this DeGreystoke Mr. Holmes?" Inspector Lestrade asked.

"When I first met the man Inspector, he had a quarter interest in the Grimthorpe Fortune. The fortune had come into the DeGreystoke Line quite by accident in the thirteenth century and included the Manor, which you have now become acquainted with. Yet, when Sir Henry Liddell, the Dean of Christ Church Oxford, spoke of him, it was as the sole heir of the entire fortune. In other words, in the course of twenty-five years, three of the four heirs of the vast fortune departed this life, and that despite each being markedly younger and more fit than Fitzwilliam DeGreystoke himself."

"A lucky man then!" declared the Constable.

"And some men make their own luck," Holmes replied, very pointedly.

"You're saying he killed the others?"

"You asked me how dangerous Mr. Fitzwilliam DeGreystoke was. I'm telling you that up to the point where he lost in both love and position to Professor Findley, he was content to follow the customs of tradition, law, and order. At that point however, like the tree I mentioned earlier, he turned away from that path. It was then that he applied his intellect to evil and became one of the most dangerous men in the Kingdom."

"Who were they Holmes, these others?"

"One was his only sibling, an elder brother named Ralph."

"He killed his own brother?" the Constable stammered.

"He wanted everything," Holmes confirmed, "a portion, even if it were millions, simply wouldn't do. You see, greed is a unique disease, unlike our other appetites greed is not appeased or satiated when it fed. Instead, the more it is served the more powerful it becomes, until it is master of all."

The Oxford Don

"You paint a black picture Mr. Holmes," the Inspector commented soberly.

"His need to kill his brother was eased by the jealousy DeGreystoke had always held against him, for the elder Ralph was as different from the younger Fitzwilliam in disposition as he was in appearance. Ralph was tall and handsome, socially at ease, charming, and outgoing. He had already laid the foundation for a bright future with his marriage to Lady Anne Fortescue, which you may recall was much in the papers at the time."

"I do," said I, "she was the daughter of Major Sir Charles Fortescue as I recall, but I couldn't have told you who the husband was."

"Indeed he was. An unfortunate riding accident while he was accompanied by his brother, his head caved in by a rock, claimed his life before he could produce an heir," Holmes finished."

"And you believe that was...our man?"

"Oh it was Inspector, undoubtedly."

"This murder of his brother preceded that of Sir Hugh DeGreystoke, first cousin to Fitzwilliam and Ralph, which occurred almost one year to the day after Ralph's...accident. The cause of the man's sudden death was never sufficiently investigated as foul play was not at first suspected and an indolent constabulary looked the other way every time."

"I remember that case," Lestrade said, "up in York. He was due to take his place in Parliament. They said he choked on his food, but it wasn't long before tongues started wagging."

"Yes, but while the lack of any evidence meant

that the case was not reopened, the whispers of suspicion soon fell upon the last surviving heir next to Fitzwilliam DeGreystoke, who by the way had departed earlier that very day. A cousin through the DeGreystoke female line, Robert Allenby, who had dined with Hugh DeGreystoke the night he died, soon garnered the suspicion while Fitzwilliam DeGreystoke remained all but invisible. The rumors were enough, we are led to believe, to blight Allenby's future and, again in about a year, he was found dead, gripping a revolver no one knew he owned in his left hand."

"A suicide?" I asked.

"It was accepted as the suicide of the presumed poisoner who used his left-hand despite being right-handed, and who still had an exceptionally bright future himself."

"Surely Mr. Holmes, DeGreystoke, if he really is as brilliant as you say he is, knew that this Allenby was right-handed," Lestrade pointed out.

"Oh he knew Inspector. There is no doubt."

"Well then, why would he have..." I began, then paused.

"That's right Watson," Holmes acknowledged, "no doubt you've understood his reason."

"He was challenging the authorities?" I said, in absolute disbelief.

"I believe he was taunting them my good fellow," Holmes replied. "Remember, he had killed at least twice before the murdering Allenby and staging it as a suicide. He had committed multiple murders and the authorities had never even suspected him. His confidence knew no bounds by that point."

"You mean it had become a sport for him?" the Inspector exclaimed.

"If he saw it as a sport or a game, such as chess, it was a lucrative one Inspector Lestrade, for it gave him the entirety of the Grimthorpe Fortune."

"And one each year until every heir but him was eliminated, odd that," Lestrade said.

"It is difficult for the disciplined mind to conduct anything in a truly random manner. The two things being so opposed to each other, when the one attempts to imitate the other it inevitably leaves its mark."

"So Fitzwilliam DeGreystoke is our man, for all of these crimes," I replied.

"Such is the danger the man presents to anyone who stands in his way," Holmes remarked.

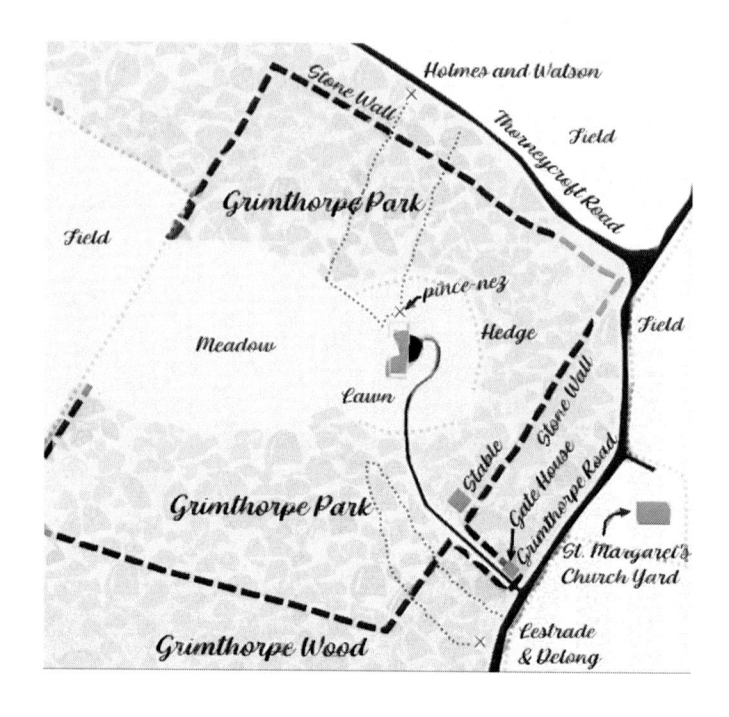

Chapter 7 – The Darkness

"I will order men for tonight," Lestrade said.

"Yes, but the locals must know nothing about any of it," Holmes warned. "We don't know who may be in league with DeGreystoke and Venner and we can't afford for them to be warned."

"No, we can't," the Inspector admitted, "and I've given the Yard the address where DeGreystoke is in hiding. Your people did well there Mr. Holmes, my compliments. They will strike the same time we do tonight, just at midnight."

"That's important," Holmes mused. "He has put a ring round him and we must take him from the

The Oxford Don

jump if we're to get him at all."

I prepared my revolver while Constable DeJong looked over the map of Grimthorpe Manor which Holmes had drawn out.

"It would prove impossible to get the evidence we need to convict him on his former murders. He had his way in those crimes and the authorities failed to press when the evidence was fresh."

"What about exhuming the body of the dead cousin? Depending upon the poison used it might still show a presence."

"But what would that show Watson?" Holmes asked. "Only that Robert Allenby, who had dined with Hugh DeGreystoke the night he died, had poisoned the latter and subsequently took his life from guilt and shame. No, the case needed energy at the start I fear and had none."

"What about his brother's death?" Lestrade asked respectfully. "You said they were together on their ride."

He was a changed man since the set-to with Holmes regarding the evidence of the pince-nez and the Morse Code message.

"True enough Inspector and had I been able to examine the scene soon afterward I would have undoubtedly been able to uncover the foul deed. Again however, DeGreystoke's explanation was accepted straightaway and no serious investigation was launched. No, he escaped from all those crimes without a stain of doubt upon his character and this emboldened him for his next great endeavor."

"The kidnapping of Professor Findley," DeJong

said.

"His revenge upon the Oxford Don," I added.

"His success made him careless however, and overly bold," Holmes added, "and from that point we've wrestled him round to the place where, in a few hours, our trap will snap shut."

"But what was the mistake Mr. Holmes?" the Constable asked curiously.

"He admitted his role in the kidnapping of Professor Findley," Holmes replied, "not only to Dr. Watson and Sherlock Holmes, mind you, but to a Scotland Yard Detective Inspector, of all things!"

"But why?"

"We'd used the man very badly, Constable," Holmes admitted, "overly bad to be honest. We'd chevied him about the train and after Dr. Watson had collared him, he shook him about like a terrier with a rat. All quite undignified really and startling. It was something he'd not experienced since he was schoolboy no doubt when the other boys harried him upon the playground. It enraged him and stirred up the old unpleasantries. Having gotten used to being treated with great reverence as a Professor over the past decades, he snapped."

"You must learn your place Mr. Holmes," I repeated. "That's what he said in the brake van."

"Yes, he had to show us that he was in control and he made it clear that he had Professor Findley."

"He called him our 'precious Oxford Don,' as I remember it Mr. Holmes," Lestrade added.

"Something like that, but if we can rescue the

Professor then we can make DeGreystoke pay."

"It'll be the rope for him then," Lestrade said, grimacing at the pain from the dog bite.

I'd given him as much laudanum as I could while still trying to keep him alert enough to oversee the Police contingent upon its arrival.

"He has earned the gallows several times over," Holmes admitted, "but he has countered every move thus far, so I tell you plainly that it will be a fortunate night's work if we are able to see our plan through to completion, but I ask you Inspector, are you going to be up to this? You seem to still be in the utmost pain."

"I'll lead my men Mr. Holmes. I won't let you down now Sir, of that you may be sure. We will storm the gate a midnight. If you and Dr. Watson make your entry with the pry bars upon the door nearest where you found the pince-nez at one- or two-minutes past, we should have drawn everything to the courtyard by then? I must admit though, I'd feel better if you had Constable DeJong with you, for he is a stout fellow."

Holmes stared from one to the other of our allies and then shook his head.

"I think not Inspector. Constable DeJong has a promising future ahead of him and tying his fate to Sherlock Holmes and Dr. John Watson in the questionable legalities regarding forced entry, could only endanger that. Your superiors usually have little tolerance for my methods, only for my results. So no, we must stay our course alone while you and your men must take the main gate and then the

Manor."

"Then a few hours' sleep is in order I think, Constable, then we will meet the men on Hart Hill Road at half-eleven," the Inspector concluded.

With that the Policemen retired to their own rooms and left Holmes and I to discuss our plan.

"Do you have everything Watson?"

"A blanket, prying bars, rope, revolver, smelling salts, long hiking staff, and the sharp knife, the ladder is outside along the storage shed."

"And the burlap bag of rocks?"

"Oh yes, a half dozen, next to the ladder."

"Well done, and now I would recommend you follow the Inspector's directions and try to get some sleep while you may. It could be a long night."

I didn't believe Holmes would sleep but I knew myself well enough not to try to keep up with my friend. His ability to tap into unseen reserves when the need was upon him was remarkable, while mine was not.

"I will wake you when the time comes."

I must have slept deeply for the hours seemed like minutes when I felt my shoulder being gently shaken.

"It's time," my friend whispered, so not to jar me awake.

This was a matter upon which I'd often accused Holmes, so it was pleasant to see so clear a change.

He had all the equipment save the ladder and the rocks arranged on the floor of his room and when I entered I couldn't help but blurt out my thoughts.

"What are you doing here?"

"I'm packing these as efficiently as possible," said he, handing me my revolver.

I placed it in my inside pocket and buttoned my jacket. Then he handed me one of the two prying bars, the smelling salts, and the tall hiking stick. I pocketed the salts and hefted the other items to get a good feel for them.

He used the knife to cut several sections of rope and laid them aside in two groups, then he sheathed the knife and slid it into his own pocket. He set the second prying bar to the side to carry. Next he laid the blanket out and placed one bundle of rope lengths inside. Finally he rolled the blanket into a long tube which he laid over one shoulder and tied together at the hip on his opposite side with one section of rope. It made a neat pack when he was done.

"I'll carry the rocks and this pry bar and we'll carry the ladder together," he said.

"Like a fire brigade," said I with a laugh, but I didn't feel much like laughing. "And what of the blanket," I asked.

"If we find Professor Findley drugged we can place him in the blanket, tying it off to the hiking staff, and carry him out," said he, confidently. "The Inspector and Constable left ten minutes ago and I think it is our time now too Watson. One last thing, we'll go in where we did last night and skirt the meadow. We'll leave the same way, avoiding that troublesome hedge."

"Good," I said, "I've got a dozen wounds thanks

to that and I'll need a new tweed suit before I'm able to go into public again."

When we reached the tool shed the moon was shining and the darkness was less oppressive than it had been the night before.

Holmes tossed me three sections of rope and three of the rocks and showed me how to secure them around the rocks.

"We'll hang these in the branches over the trail in case anyone pursues us, it will give them...pause."

"I'll say," grimacing at the thought of taking one of the stones to the head at a full run on a dark trail.

We made our way quietly up the main road and out of Stalisfield Green onto Thorneycroft Road, then east to our entry point in the woods the night before. Had anyone glimpsed us they would have had a hard time concluding that we were anything but burglars bent upon mischief, but going over the tall stone wall by the ladder was much easier than climbing for it as we'd done. Once on top I pulled the ladder up and lowered it down the opposite side to where Holmes had dropped a moment earlier. We then spent the next twenty minutes carrying the ladder down the path and tying the ropes with rocks off on higher branches. Finally we returned to the wall and placed the ladder up in our place of escape and made our way back out to the meadow, minding the new hazards we'd put up at head height.

"Half-Eleven," Holmes muttered quietly as we crouched in the shadows of the forest along the verge and looked out upon the moonlit meadow where, here and there, a few red deer grazed in peace for once, the mastiffs being put up for the night.

We watched the old pile for any movement but just then some clouds began to move over the moon, casting new and eerie shadows across the lawns.

"I see nothing at all," Holmes said.

"Nor I. All is still although occasionally I hear the deer moving about."

"Wait!" Holmes whispered frantically. "What is that? Do you see it, just there?"

He pointed to the far end of the Manor where a three-story tower had been added on at some point across the ages.

"Two men," he hissed. "Do you see them?"

"Standing perfectly still?" I asked. "Are those men or young trees?"

"Surely they are men," said he, "but these clouds are making it difficult to tell."

"If they are men Holmes we'll never get to the door let alone get it open without them discovering us."

"You are correct Watson," said he, gravely, "so I must find out. Only fifteen minutes left so you will have to make your way to the door alone. I will lead them away if they are men but if they are simply trees I'll join you straightaway."

He gave me a confident nod and then he did something I'd never seen my friend, nor any other human for that matter, do. Sherlock Holmes began loping across the open meadow with long strides on all fours. His silhouette cast a shape not much different than a huge wolf or hound would have done but the sound of his going was much more substantial and in a moment I saw the trees move. Holmes had been correct. Two men were pointing and talking surprisingly loudly and then, to my horror, the sound of a rifle crackled through the calm night sky, causing the red deer to leap and flee at full speed into the safety of the dark woods. When I looked back to where Holmes had been there was nothing, no sound, no movement, no shadows and no Sherlock Holmes.

My heart raced as I thought of my friend lying wounded out there in the meadow and I nearly took to my feet to go in search of him. I barely stopped myself in time as I saw the two men, obviously armed, moving out into the tall, wild grass of the meadow. It was my time and I needed to go but a sick, nauseous feeling came over me and I paused.

"Go Watson! Go!" a voice hissed to me and in a moment Holmes came crawling out of the grass. "They'll be but a few minutes," he whispered, "go!"

Then we were off, hunched low and moving as quietly as it was possible to do. We were at least two minutes late arriving on the shadowy northern side of Grimthorpe Manor where Holmes had found the golden pince-nez the night before.

"Here Watson," Holmes called quietly, "press to and I'll keep watch," he added, breathing heavily from his wild lope across the meadow.

That escapade had taken it out of him and he was glad of a moment to catch his breath. I went to it with my pry bar as quietly as I could but the gap between the door and the frame was too tight to hold the tip and it continued to slide free.

"Holmes," I called, "it requires both of us pressing in turns so the other can push the tip farther in."

Finally I had a strong hold and was ready to force the door when Holmes' strong grip seized me by the arm and nearly paralyzed me.

"Silence!" he barely breathed.

I held perfectly still while the two men came and stood not a dozen feet from us.

"It was a wolf I tell you. No dog moves like that," the first voice said. It wasn't either of the voices I'd heard from Venner or Creighton the day before.

"You're a fool Tom Jolley, there hay'nt been

wolves round here in a hundert years or more. T'were all hunted out," the second voice said.

"What's the shootin' about?" someone yelled out a window two floors directly above us. It was the voice of Cuthbert Creighton.

"Old Jolley thought he saw a wolf!"

Before anything more could be said a great din was heard in the direction of the front gate and Creighton ordered the men there immediately. The window was then slammed shut and the sound of running feet retreated quickly into the darkness.

"Now Watson, Now!" Holmes cried, careless of the sound.

I bent to with all my weight and strength to the splintering sound of good old English Oak echoed across the lawn as the frame and door splintered around the lock. I fell forward as the door itself flew open and the warm air inside rushed over me.

Holmes helped me to my feet and then rushed into the dimly lit hall that soon turned right in the shadows ahead. A moment later I could hear the splintering of more oak and by the time I reached him, my friend was standing with his back to the door and looking down onto the body of what I first took to be a child.

"Professor," said he, shaking him. "Professor Findley!"

Holmes unslung the blanket without a pause and cast it about the floor, tying corners and the center to the pole with flying fingers. Then he laid the little man down and folded the blanket over, completing the task in double-quick-time.

The Oxford Don

I took of my end, surprised at how light the man's body felt, and we retraced our steps out into the night. The cool air was invigorating and we jogged out boldly, hoping that everyone was still occupied with the Police, although the noise from that quarter had died down. We passed the end of the thick hedge and rushed along the edge of the meadow as fast as we dared in the darkness. Holmes was trusting me to find our path back through the woods and I was on high alert.

"Here," I called, pointing with my free hand as

we left the meadow and launched ourselves into the woods of Grimthorpe Park once more.

We hadn't gone fifty feet when a specter stepped from the shadows and out into the moonlit trail, barring our way. It was George Venner and he held a rifle or shotgun in one hand and the leash of a huge mastiff, glowing eerily in the bright rays of the moon.

"You've undone us," he said in a weary voice, "but don't think you'll live to see the fruits of your handiwork Gentlemen. Your road ends here."

Before I could pull my revolver or even drop the litter we carried the Oxford Don in, the devil dropped the leash and gave the giant hound the command to attack.

To our shock and George Venner's horror the animal simply sat down and yawned. I had no time to consider the strange behavior for at that instant Holmes flashed past me and took the man down at a full run. The two rolled this way and that upon the ground, each vying for the upper hand, but the dog paid them no attention at all and simply continued to stare at the moon. Stepping forward cautiously I moved to the spot where Venner seemed to be gaining the upper hand and stuck him upon head with my revolver handle.

"Oh well played Watson, well played," Holmes cried as he threw Venner's unconscious body to the side of the trail. He was at the top of his game and filled with excitement as he jumped to his feet. It was a state I had more than once described as positively canine. We bound and gagged the man with pleasure and rolled him over unceremoniously into the brush off to the side of the trail.

"Remember Watson, we're nearly upon the hanging rocks so go low my friend, go low."

This trick made carrying even the slight form of Professor Findley that much more difficult and we were nearly to the ladder when we heard a series of screams emanating just from the woods behind us. These horrifying shrieks were followed by silence and as I climbed the ladder to the top of the wall and took hold of our litter Holmes smiled at the sudden silence of the night.

"It looks like at least a few fellows have found our rocks Watson," said he with an obvious satisfaction in his voice.

"I hope it wasn't the Police," I said.

"Never fear," he cried as he reached the ground and took his end of the litter, "the Police have lanterns!"

An hour later Holmes and I had snuck silently back into the Plough and Professor Malcolm Findley had been tucked comfortably into Holmes' bed to sleep off the drug.

"The dog was obviously drugged," Holmes said, as we sat and looked upon his former tutor and mentor. "No doubt with the professor's food."

"But I also found traces of injections upon his arm," I replied, "so they used both methods."

"That would explain it then," said he, "why he was unconscious when we found him."

"It's probably just as well Holmes," I confided, "for the occurrences of the night could only have been upsetting to him."

By morning Professor Findley was conscious and hungry. Holmes had stayed up through the night watching over the man and hoping for some news on the happenings at Grimthorpe Manor and in London, but as of breakfast we'd as yet heard nothing. Nor for that matter had we seen Inspector Lestrade or Constable DeJong.

As we sat at the table awaiting the arrival of our food and watching a sunny day developing outside, the Professor finally began to speak freely.

"It was awfully good of you fellows to see me clear of that dismal place, but I say Sherlock, you are looking most frightfully thin man. What have you been doing with yourself?"

"I'm afraid I may have been spending myself a little too freely Professor," Holmes said, a kindly smile playing about his lips.

"Well, it was good of you fellows just the same."

"What do you know of Professor De Greystoke and his plans," I asked.

"A capital fellow that," replied the little man, confusing me to no end.

"You are speaking of the man who kidnapped you from your classroom?" I asked. "Ostensibly to kill you."

"Well, yes, quite, I suppose," said he, the words tumbling out of him as he sipped the freshly arrived cup of hot coffee. "There is that."

I looked to Holmes for some clarification but he only smiled weakly and took up his own cup.

"A capital fellow for all that?" I asked.

"Setting aside the deep, malignant tendencies alive in him today, Dr. Watson," said he, "he really is a most brilliant man. Why I recall upon our first meeting how he..."

The man's words continued in some uplifting story about which I couldn't tell you so much as a sentence. My mind was numb at the thought that there was no overarching sense of wrong in Holmes' former tutor. He didn't even seem to be afraid and that despite having just spent a good deal of time as a kidnapped man, drugged, imprisoned, and facing his death at the hands of an old friend. How could such a thing be, I pondered.

After we finished our breakfast and adjourned to Holmes' rooms Inspector Lestrade finally joined us.

"I'm glad to find you looking so well Professor," said he, as he limped in and looked at the man.

"And I thank you for all your labors to make it so Inspector...Lestrade did you say Holmes? Yes, my sincerest thanks and please convey my deepest appreciation to your men as well for I know they fought for me as well."

"It was a bit of a struggle there at the Manor," Lestrade said, understating the battle they'd faced to enter the Barbican and take the Castle.

"How many?" Holmes asked, mysteriously.

"We took a dozen roughs Mr. Holmes, that is including Mr. Creighton and George Venner. We found the latter out on the trail with three others, those hanging rocks were deadly in the dark. Laid those men out flat they did. Pretty smart that. I did have a half dozen of my lads injured in storming of the castle, but no losses. They'll have to see the doctor of course, but that beats the mortician as we say. It was a hard-fought thing to be sure for whoever it was who designed the place knew what they were about. No doubts there."

"And London?" Holmes asked, when Lestrade didn't volunteer the information immediately.

"London," said he. "We got Mr. Jack Fothergill and four others, a bad lot if you ask me. Some long records among them."

"But DeGreystoke?" Holmes insisted.

It was so obvious that Lestrade was trying to evade saying it, but finally he was forced to admit the unfortunate outcome.

"He gave us the slip Mr. Holmes. I still don't know how he managed but there it is. I won't know more until I'm back in London."

Holmes rose, went to the window, and stared out until the Inspector finally realized that he wasn't going to turn around.

"Well, I need to return to London Gentlemen, so I'll be wishing you well Professor, Dr. Watson..." his words faded away and he took his leave.

"What now Holmes?" I asked.

"Now we must get this man to a telegraph office so he can notify his wife, then I suppose..." Holmes paused.

"Yes, I suppose you're correct Sherlock. It's time to put a stop to Professor DeGreystoke."

Chapter 8 – The Matchstick Message

"You do know that if you pursue him, he will prove...quite deadly?" Professor Findley pointed out while relaxing upon our settee at 221B.

"I expected as much," Holmes replied. "It's something we've become hardened to over time, is it not Watson?"

"Indeed Professor," I admitted, "we tend to deal with men at their most dangerous."

"Yes, quite, however, they have not been...him, you know, have they Sherlock?"

"True," Holmes acknowledged, "but thankfully

there is only one Fitzwilliam DeGreystoke."

"And he will seek to kill you, both of you."

"As he would have killed you Professor?" I asked the obvious, "for that was his plan was it not?"

It was strange to see the deference with which Holmes treated our guest and I only slowly realized the important part the little man had played in my friend's life.

"No doubt you're correct Dr. Watson, had he been able to isolate me without detection, he would have savored my slow demise very much I suspect. We must acknowledge, however, that I have been the chief antagonist of his strained existence and one must make allowances."

"Allowances?" I cried in disbelief, "for your would-be murderer?"

"For my fellow man Doctor, who but for some pulse deep in the cosmos might well have been me. After all, gaining the love of my beautiful wife and a place of honor in my college were never guarantees. Her own father, for instance, strongly preferred another candidate for her hand, and our Dean at the time had expressed a marked preference for Fitzwilliam for the open position, did you know? So but for the grace of God," said he.

"But surely your charity knows some bounds does it not? For you will not try to convince me now that had DeGreystoke won her hand and the position at your college, that you would have plotted his kidnapping and murder."

"A gentleman knows the bounds to be sure and no, I would not have sought his death had our roles been reversed. Have you not found though, that there is no one so boorish as a man void of charity. I've often noticed that those who place themselves above their fellow man and hold themselves as coldly and unbendingly superior are the most miserable people to be around. They are the most unhappy of souls."

"I understand Professor Findley, I am only shocked by your attitude toward the man who kidnapped you with the goal of killing you and who, if the evidence is to be believed, still hopes to take your life."

"My allowances and, if you will, my charity toward the man who was once, and for many years, a dear friend, does not diminish his guilt. It cannot. It does, however, mean that I cannot forget that he was once important to me. That he must answer for his actions is something I could not and would not attempt to resist. I suppose I must even join in the crusade to take him, now that you have saved me, but I can never find anything but sorrow in the downfall of my old friend. That he was once such a bright, shining thing in my estimation, such a rare man among men, only means that my sorrow must be compounded. This is my definition of the charity I feel for him, but as I said, I suppose I must now become a part of the effort to bring him down."

"It would be best, Professor, otherwise," Holmes replied, "you'd have to be hedged about by police to insure your safety, until we finally took him."

"I will be most dreadfully underfoot, for you well know that my strengths are not on the ground, so to speak."

"The theoretical can sometimes be as valuable as the practical, although we will doubtless be moving quickly if I remember De Greystoke's methods accurately."

"He does love the dramatic," Professor Findley said, looking intensely at Holmes, "like someone else I know."

"Yes, it was ever a temptation," Holmes replied, "and one which I continue to indulge from time to time I'm afraid."

"And you know...he loves to be in control and dictate the action. Alas, the chess board was never his only stage."

"His nature as well as his stature, will both be difficult for him to mask," said Holmes.

"But not impossible...as to the latter he will no doubt use a wheelchair and, with a false riser to increase his height...and padded legs to give the impression of fullness, he will appear a much larger man."

"And with padded shoulders to suggest breadth and muscle," Holmes added, "he may very well succeed in passing himself, despite his size, off as someone altogether different."

"His beard will disappear but he will not submit completely to necessity," the Professor announced. "It is impossible for the man to bow completely to anything or anyone, even to the forces of necessity. A flamboyant moustache of some sort will be kept as a compromise between his proud nature and the wisest course of action."

"And the more formal, worsted wool suits will be sacrificed, wouldn't you think?"

"Indeed Sherlock, for tweeds no doubt."

"And his manservant?"

"Hired from Neibaum's, most likely."

"No doubt," Holmes agreed, referring to one of the large agencies for gentlemen's gentlemen.

All of these deductions had poured out in less than a minute, leaving me struggling to keep up. It was very much like the interactions I'd witnessed between Sherlock and his own brother, Mycroft, without the edge of competition, however.

"And he will not be a seasoned valet, but quite inexperienced," Professor Findley remarked.

"Because DeGreystoke will not want him to perform all the standard duties."

"Precisely, no doubt he will be kept well out of the secrets and serve as a minder more than a valet, a pusher of the wheelchair and a retriever of this and that. Someone to run the errands."

"And the carriage?"

"A Haldane Coach. You've heard of it, no?"

"No," Holmes admitted, clearly feeling strange to not know something regarding the streets and roads of London while Professor Findley did.

"It's been around twenty-odd years, the clever invention of another Scot, Haldane by name, from Kinross. It's a Brougham Carriage modified with a ramp that stows away underneath the carriage and has fold up seats, either of which can form a cutout for the wheelchair while the other is used by a passenger, side-by-side. Quite convenient really."

"And how is it you came to know of it?" Holmes asked, curiously.

"Lord Agnew purchased one several years back, swears by the thing. You remember Lord Agnew, no? Well, he attends Christ Church Cathedral each Sunday and suffers terribly from the sciatica."[26]

"I imagine such an invention spares him from great pain," I said, knowing what kind of suffering such patients endured.

"It saves him four horrifically painful transfers to and from his chair for each trip he must take."

"It will be simple to investigate the sales and rentals of the coaches and have my irregulars search them out," Holmes offered.

"But will DeGreystoke not understand your reasoning and simply counter it, after all he saw

---

[26] Sciatica was believed a rheumatic condition in the Victorian Era. "Rheumatism, Rheumatic Gout and Sciatica," by William Henry Fuller, pub. John Churchill, London, ©1852. Source: British Journal of Anesthesia, October 2007, by M. A. Stafford, P. Peng & D. A. Hill.

through your disguise of the brush salesman on the train and that is a great...rarity," I declared.

"He very well could Dr. Watson," the little professor agreed amicably, "and your point is well made, that he should realize what we are thinking. Yet there is an undeniable phenomena at work in many of our most brilliant minds. Call it a most unfortunate 'inclination' if you will. I'll liken it to the case of injury in large dogs. Have you ever noticed, for instance, the high number of large dogs suffering from shoulder and hip problems in later life."

"Dogs!" I exclaimed, confused. "But what does such an ailment in dogs have to do with unfortunate inclinations in those with superior intellects?"

"Most large dogs are overactive in their youth, while their bodies are still in the developmental stage, and injure themselves. While they don't show the ultimate effects of those injuries until later in life, the damage was most certainly done in their youth."

"In the same way," the Professor continued on, "some brilliant minds, mainly among those who've experience success acclaim from early in their lives, develop the notion that the vast majority of the mankind are little more than certifiable idiots. With such an outlook they unconsciously and habitually underate those they view as intellectual inferiors."

"But how can he view Holmes in that way? He was beaten by him in chess, of all things, then played to a stalemate."

"Yes Watson, but as I said, I don't believe Mr. DeGreystoke recalls that event or if he does, then at least not the part I played in it."

Haldane's Modified Carriage-Coach

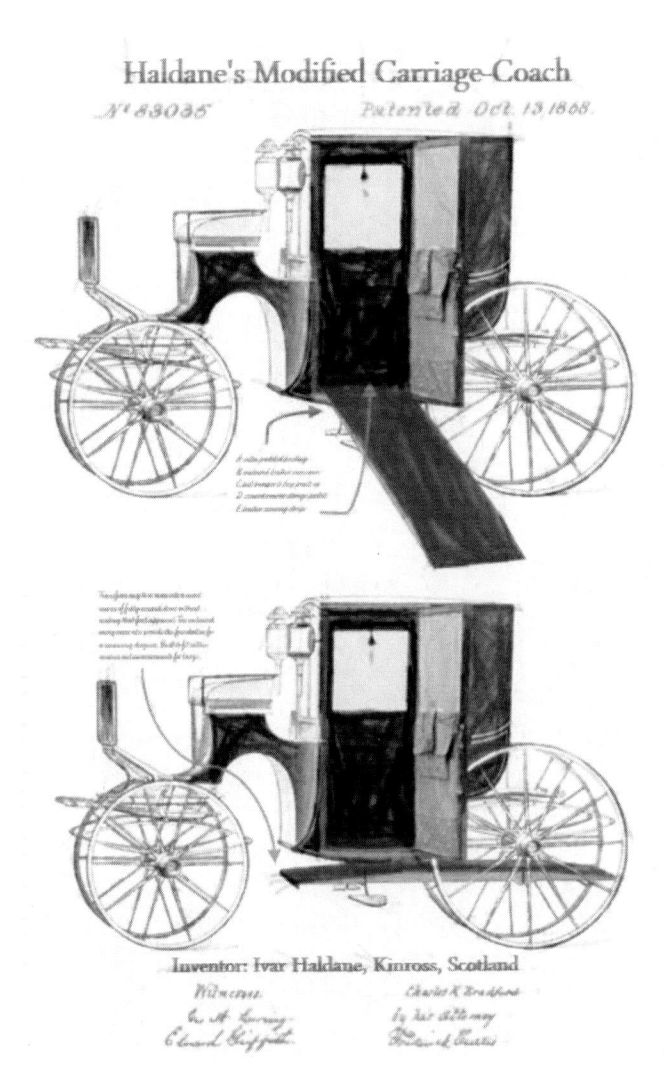

Inventor: Ivar Haldane, Kinross, Scotland

"And if I may say so Dr. Watson, without giving offence, considering the extensive exposure which Sherlock's career has received through the prism of your stories, delightful as my wife and I find them, I believe Fitzwilliam will view him as terribly plebian and, therefore, no real threat."

By "plebian" Professor Findley meant common or lower class, as opposed to being an international chess champion I presumed. While I knew what he was saying about my stories I could find nothing at all common, either in my friend's many remarkable abilities or in the amazing results he'd achieved in what was now dozens of cases.

"So he won't believe that Holmes could deduce his actions?"

"Precisely Watson," said Holmes, "and if you recall, our acting talents convinced DeGreystoke that he'd defeated us upon the train. He is a man with a great deal of confidence and pride."

"Will he not see through to your helping us Professor Findley?" I asked.

"While Fitzwilliam didn't doubt my intelligence I'm afraid he always saw me as what he referred to disparagingly as a 'textbook intellectual.' You heard me admit that my strengths were not on the ground, so to speak, and I assure you Doctor that I was not expressing any kind of false humility. As a speaker on philosophical topics my old friend would have put his money on me every time, but in the world of competitive chess I lacked both the killer instinct as well as the ability to cope with the abruptness of it all, especially in light of the quite arbitrary time limitations which some ill-advised people have managed to foist upon the game."

I shook my head at all the notions I'd just heard. Some things made little enough sense to me but I let them go. If, as was often the case, things became clearer as we went along, I'd understand soon enough. To say that trying to keep up with Professor Findley and Sherlock Holmes at the same time was not more than a little dizzying would have been an understatement.

"He'll assume you are here with us." I said.

"And he'll purchase new subalterns to be sure."[27]

"Most of his gang is in a London prison but money isn't an issue for him so we can expect spies soon Watson."

"I'll warn Mrs. Watson," I volunteered, "so she isn't taken in by the odd repairman or salesman."

"And I'll see to Billy and the Irregulars," Holmes added.

"If he realizes we've seen through his disguise he will lose no time on procuring another," the Oxford Don warned. "And what the next one would be is not so easy to predict."

"My people act with a certain...circumspection, I assure you Professor," Holmes said, with his usual flair.

"How certain are you, Professor," I asked, "of your deductions regarding DeGreystoke?" I asked.

"How sure are you, Dr. Watson, of your ability to predict how your friend here might respond in various...situations?" said he, gesturing at Holmes.

"Quite certain, I would venture."

"And you have known Sherlock what, less than

---

[27] Lieutenants to work on one's behalf. In military parlance an officer of lower rank than captain.

a decade? Whereas I, Malcolm Findley, have known my old friend Fitzwilliam DeGreystoke since I was little more than a boy and for nearly a half-century now."

His point was well taken and I was thankful he made no comparison of his intellect with my own, to drive his point home even more powerfully.

"And as to your...stories, Dr. Watson. I would take a moment to assure you that the faculty of Christ Church College places such a value upon each of them that whenever a new one is published my dear wife arranges a soiree at our residence to celebrate the event. At which time our Orator, the right honorable Ignatius Crowley, always has the honor of reading it out in its entirety without pause or interruption of any kind."[28]

Then, to my surprise, the man continued by speaking of the rocks we'd hung upon the trail.

"And did you know that Holmes had gotten his idea for hanging rocks along the trails of Grimthorpe Park from my description of my old home upon the Isle of Lewis? It lies among the islands in the windswept northwest of Scotland, where the only way for us to keep our thatched roof from blowing away in the gales was by holding it in place with a net of ropes weighted at the ends by just such stones as you used upon that dark trails at Grimthorpe."

"It provided us some additional time to make our escape," Holmes admitted with a guilty smile.

"You see Doctor, the mind not only creates what has never existed, it also synthesizes solutions from what already exists."

"So," I reasoned out loud, "when someone decides that most of their fellow men are certifiable idiots...they also underestimate our ability to learn from what is already around us."

The little man was delighted that I'd understood

---

[28] The position of Orator or Public Orator is an historical one at Oxford and Cambridge dating back to the 1500's. Their duties include speech writing, speeches during royal or honorary visitations, and the general representation of their respective university through public addresses upon fitting occasions.

his point without further explanation.

"My dear wife Queenie, or rather, Amitas née Wycliffe-Ward, will find it fascinating that I was able to visit with the author of the Sherlock Holmes' Stories. How curious she will be about you Sir, and she will ask me a thousand questions which I did not think to ask you when I was in company with you, and so had the chance. I shall be scolded; I have no doubt."

The man's sincerity was touching, although I found it difficult to imagine soirees being held in honor of my stories, soirees at which the university Orator himself was proud to serve as story-reader.

"You may tell her she has my permission to write me with any question you are unable to answer to her satisfaction Professor, that way you may escape her disappointment," I said humorously.

His eyes shined at the thought of it and I wondered how seriously I could take him. Was this all a great joke to the little man or was he as sincere as I thought he was?

Billy entered almost upon cue and Inspector Lestrade, lean and furtive as ever, followed a second later.

"Gentlemen," said he, acknowledging us. "We checked that address Mr. Holmes, the one from the trunk on the train, 305 Charing Cross, and there was nothing."

"There were no clues?" Holmes asked.

"There was nothing at all. A dusty, bare-planked floor with not a stick of furniture to mention, and obviously closed up for a long time by the look."

The Oxford Don

"An apartment?"

"An office with a few rooms attached."

"And there was nothing at all in any of the rooms? You are quite sure."

"There was but an unused matchstick laying upon the dusty windowsill Mr. Holmes, but that hardly..."

"Do you have it?" Holmes interrupted with that sleuthhound energy of his. "And did you happen to notice that while the windowsill was quite dusty, the matchstick was not?"

Lestrade's confused expression said it all and when he produced the item in question Holmes grabbed it without ceremony, bypassed his convex lens, and raced straight to his microscope.

"Watson," he cried a moment later, "look at this will you!"

We all gathered around and I looked through the lens showing one of the four sides of the matchstick, which as Holmes had pointed out was clean and free of dust.

"I have sacrificed my," I read aloud from a series of miniscule etchings in the wood.

"Now roll it forward to the next side Watson, away from you," Holmes directed.

"rook and you think," I read, then rolled it forward again. "you are winning" On the fourth and final side I read, "CHECK MATE!"

Holmes had been pacing feverishly up and down behind us as I read out the messages on the sides of the matchstick and now he stopped and said it aloud in its entirety.

"I have sacrificed my rook and you think you are winning - CHECK MATE!"

The excitement was gone from my friend and he stared at Professor Findley and shook his head with an expression of puzzling sorrow. I had apparently missed the point of the message completely for I saw no reason in any of it which might account for my friend's sadness.

"Did you come in a cab Inspector?" Holmes asked.

"No Sir, in the police carriage."

"Then be so good as to call down from the window and dismiss him, would you?"

"If you insist Mr. Holmes."

"I'm afraid I must Inspector."

Lestrade was as confused as me but he did as he'd been instructed and, closing the window, he turned to Holmes.

"I hope you'll explain yourself Mr. Holmes?"

Professor Findley had resumed his seat upon the settee and Holmes handed me a quickly written note.

"Tack that to the door will you Dr. Watson," he said in a strange formal manner.

"STAY AWAY!" it said in large letters. "STAY WELL AWAY!" Then it was signed, "Sherlock Holmes."

"What is the meaning of all this?" I demanded when I returned.

"I'm afraid that Professor Findley is carrying a disease Watson, although what it might be escapes my view at present. I need you to examine him most thoroughly if you would."

"And that's why you had me send the carriage away Mr. Holmes?" Lestrade asked, gravely.

"I'm afraid so Inspector and depending upon what Dr. Watson finds, we might be here a while."

I was gripped with a great dread at Holmes' words, for it had not been that long since Cholera had ravaged London and bodies were taken away in carts.[29] Russia, Germany, and France were even now suffering under that terrible disease and we still had no cure as far as I was aware.[30] At Professor Findley's age too, I worried that such a thing could easily prove fatal. That Fitzwilliam DeGreystoke could have meant what Holmes had hinted at, that his former tutor might be infected, was diabolical. The evil behind such a thing, if that was indeed what those words, "I have sacrificed my rook and you think you are winning – checkmate," might mean, was impossible for me to comprehend.

I retrieved my bag and began my examination with a heavy heart.

"Are you saying that DeGreystoke went beyond simply drugging the Professor?" Lestrade asked.

"A poison would have made its presence known by now, whereas a disease might take time to show itself. This is why I feared the latter when I read the matchstick message," Holmes said, soberly. "The decision to infect the Professor meant that De Greystoke no longer had to worry about keeping

---

[29] London's final Cholera outbreak took place in 1866.
[30] The fifth international cholera outbreak of the 1800's lasted from 1881 through 1896, claiming 500,000.

him out of our hands, that became a moot point."

"He would be carrying his own death sentence, in that case, and we could do nothing for him," the Inspector muttered under his breath as he returned to stare miserably out the window.

When we rescued him from Grimthorpe Manor we'd put Professor Findley's weakness down to his being drugged, but now I wondered. I found his forehead cool to the touch and upon closer examination a slight bluish tinge to the skin under his eyes, both symptoms of the dreaded disease.

"Have you experienced weakness, vomiting, or diarrhea?" I asked.

"Yes Doctor, but I believed that was my body's response to the drugs I'd been given, either through injections or in my food or water."

I nodded and smiled reassuringly but the details I'd observed pointed to a grim prognosis, the man lying motionless upon the settee and staring at me with sunken, listless eyes and, by his own judgment, unusually wrinkled hands, had contracted cholera and was suffering from life threatening dehydration. The end usually came quickly after this. Beyond this, his weakened state and upset digestion were symptoms as well.

"What do you think Watson?" Holmes finally asked.

"Do not spare my feelings Doctor, for I want to know the truth of the matter."

Every eye was turned upon me but I was loathe to speak for the main reason that I had no solution to offer with my diagnosis.

"Professor Findley has definitely been infected with cholera," I announced. "His symptoms are of the full range and so advanced that I would say it had to have occurred early after his kidnapping."

"What medicine do you need?" Lestrade asked, eager to help.

"I know of none that are effective," I admitted, sadly, "but I know a physician who has specialized in this disease."

Holmes immediately called for Billy to come up, stopping him at the top of the steps.

"Dr. Robert Stanley," I said from the door, "at 18 Sackville Street, tell him Dr. John Watson requires his help."

With that the lad was off in a flash and I watched him race up the street in search of a cab.

"You know this man?" Holmes asked.

"We were classmates," I replied, "but while I went to the Army he opened his own practice."

"But he understands the disease?" Holmes inquired again.

"Far better than I do," I reassured, "but some of his methods are controversial and he does not hold to the accepted miasma theory, that it is spread by noxious air. Oh, and he has written a monograph upon the subject as well Holmes, and even issued an updated edition."

Holmes was regularly writing monographs upon his latest views and theories and I thought he might respect a fellow specialist who did the same.

Meanwhile Lestrade had taken to pacing up and down as Holmes had done earlier, wringing his hands and looking constantly at the clock. He'd visited us a hundred times but he'd never felt himself trapped in 221B before, let alone with a man infected with Cholera.

"What do we have to say of a man who would use such a method to commit murder and perhaps even start an epidemic?" I asked.

"He is a deadly menace to be sure," Professor Findley replied.

"And it isn't beyond plausible that he believed he might actually infect others," Holmes added.

"Namely us?" Lestrade commented.

"Precisely us," Holmes agreed.

"Well I remember the wagons in the streets," the Inspector fairly hissed, "filled with the dead bodies in East London they were and I swear I'll hunt this man down with the greatest satisfaction."

"You mean, if we get the chance," Holmes said.

"Well yes, quite."

When the door opened and a balding man with heavy sideburns and thick eyebrows walked in with an armload of medical equipment, followed by a strongly built nurse carrying his case and other supplies, we were all shocked. They left the door open and the smell of disinfectant wafted in on the air behind them.

"John," he called out, "This is Nurse Chadwick and Nurse Donnelly is wiping down everything from your front handrails, doorknobs and knocker, all the way through your establishment. Your page took his own disinfecting under protest, you might say, but we are done with him. You gentlemen must move back. Yes, sit there at the table until nurse is able to see to you."

With this Holmes and Lestrade obediently took seats at our table and waited.

"And this is the patient?" Dr. Stanley said as he arranged a metal pole behind the settee. It had a rack to hold an upturned bottle of a clear liquid.

"Professor Findley," I said, noticing that the little man had grown markedly less responsive just in the short time since I'd completed my examination.

"A simple saline solution to augment the blood," Stanley said, pointing to the upturned bottle. "The oxygenated salts restore the vitality to the blood."

"His pulse was weak and grew weaker," I said, "and his breathing is heavy. The wrinkling of the hands was abnormal, the Professor noted, and the skin about his face was cool to the touch and had gained a bluish tinge."

"Very helpful John," said he, "and if you could just come over and continue to monitor his pulse and breathing as I see to injecting the needle."

I did as I was bid, happy to be of service and learn the latest technique for dealing with the disease from my former classmate.

Even as I saw the drops of saline water begin down the tube the renewed smell of disinfectant hit me in a powerful wave. Holmes and Lestrade were now having their hands, faces, sleeves and cuffs, and even shoes sanitized.

"And you Gentlemen?" Dr. Stanley asked, turning upon them.

"I live here," Holmes offered.

"And I don't," Lestrade said.

After a battery of questions which were all answered in the negative, and as the other nurse entered and saw to the cleaning of the doorknob and general area, Lestrade was given his liberty. He left without pause, no doubt feeling fortunate that he hadn't fallen under the painful reign of a quarantine, as he'd fully expected.

"I'll be in contact...by telegram," he said from the door.

"His pulse has grown much stronger," I said in complete amazement.

"Good," Dr. Stanley said as he checked his watch. "Right on track Nurse Chadwick."

"Now John," said he, "I must determine where this man contracted the disease."

Chapter 9 – Devilish!

"I must admit I was in error as to what Professor DeGreystoke's next move might be Watson, which is I fear a more common occurrence than your good readers may realize," Holmes said, as our cab took us across London. "I never saw the possibility of his infecting Professor Findley with Cholera. It was a failing of imagination, a thing I've long condemned in others."

"What sane man could have foreseen such a thing?" I insisted. "The very idea is...devilish Holmes, absolutely devilish."

I had begun to see a kind of nobility in the understanding approach Holmes' former tutor had taken with his adversary, but I confess that this latest development painted all such higher sentiment as utter foolishness where Fitzwilliam DeGreystoke was concerned.

I recalled that moment when we realized what DeGreystoke had done and the expression upon Holmes' usually indiscernible face. It had been one of horror, for Cholera was not only a virtual death sentence for his old tutor, but it also held out the real possibility of an agonizing death for thousands more innocent Londoners with us among them.

Even Holmes, who prided himself on gaining a knowledge of his adversary's mind in order to predict their actions, had been unable to put himself as low as DeGreystoke had become.

Lestrade had put a man with Professor Findley, whose condition continued to improve with the oxygenated salts, and Dr. Stanley said he would look in twice daily. He was as horrified as we had been to hear how his patient had contracted the disease and had Scotland Yard not already been intricately involved in the case he would no doubt have demanded it. As it was he satisfied himself with keeping Nurse Chadwick on hand to push plenty of good food and water upon the man and to see to the thorough disinfecting of the area.

"What had you foreseen?"

The Oxford Don

"I believed he would, under the guise of the wheelchair-bound man, attempt to retake his man."

"Whom he sees as our 'King'," I replied.

"Indeed Watson, but when I read the matchstick message about us believing we were winning when we were actually facing a checkmate, I realized that whatever DeGreystoke had done he'd had made the recapture of the Oxford Don unnecessary. That was when I grasped that matters were for more grave than any of us could have dreamed."

Our cab dropped us in a back alley in the better part of town, where fine homes faced the front street and vied with their neighbors for attention.

Lestrade, himself nursing what Holmes so often called that "lean and hungry look" as well as suffering from his recent tête-à-tête with the hounds of Grimthorpe, was standing in the open door of the servant's entrance at the rear of one of Curzon Street's finer residences."[31]

"The owners have given us access to this place, but I have to say that this case makes my blood boil Gentlemen," he remarked. "It is the lowest crime of anything I've ever seen in all my years."

"It does reorder the criminal world somewhat, does it not?" Holmes offered.

"It does Mr. Holmes. Casts a new light upon our criminal classes. Makes the simple murderer seem almost sane and merciful by comparison, wouldn't you agree?"

---

[31] "Yond Cassius has a lean and hungry look," Shakespeare's Julius Caesar, Act 1, Scene 2, 190–195.

"It does," I agreed, even though the thought of it seemed ludicrous.

"I have said before Gentlemen," Holmes said, "that there is nothing new under the sun, that it has all been done before, however, I cannot recall another crime like this one."

I contemplated my friend's sobering words as

Lestrade led us inside and up the servants winding back stairs of a fine home.

Despite all we'd seen, and that was a great deal actually, as my notes confirmed, DeGreystoke's actions were diabolically unique in all the annals.

"Is that Curzon Street before us Inspector?"

"The address you supplied us Mr. Holmes, 118 Curzon Street. Your people did well and we've seen the carriage you described."

"Holmes," I called that instant. "Look!"

Sherlock Holmes stepped up to the window, which had only a sheer curtain drawn, and deftly released a telescope from his cane and drew it to his eye.[32]

"That is our man Gentleman," he said after a minute, "even without his beard I recognize him."

As a young man left the carriage and arranged the ramp on the far side Holmes handed each of us his telescope in turn.

"That's the devil," Lestrade growled.

"Indeed!" I said, shocked to see the man so clearly through the glass. It was obviously the same man and where the wild beard had once grown a thick, lustrous moustache now spread across the face.

"Are your men ready?" Holmes asked.

"Just awaiting my signal Mr. Holmes," Lestrade said, pulling a bright red silk handkerchief from his pocket.

"You can take him now then," Holmes said, but

---

[32] Dolland of London, maker of fine optical equipment, founded 1750. Marine Telescope Cane, circa 1880.

even before Lestrade could step to the window there was a great commotion and the carriage raced off down Curzon Street leaving the valet and the ramp upon the walk.

"What happened?" Lestrade cried, pulling the sheer curtain aside with a jerk.

"He recognized a policeman," Holmes said, staring down upon the street. "That one, there," he pointed, "the one crossing the street at an odd angle and on a direct line with where DeGreystoke's carriage was sitting."

"There would have been no reason for him to take such an angle to cross the street," I noted.

"An excellent observation Watson, but if he were a policeman there would be a reason, just one though, and that would be to ensnare the devil."

Lestrade was beside himself and nearly catatonic as he dropped into one of the fine chairs.

Holmes sat down as well, returning his scope to the hollow tube atop his cane he replaced the golden knob back to its place.

"What's to be done now Mr. Holmes," the Inspector barely whispered, his head still slumped upon his chest.

"While this was unfortunate," Holmes said, "it wasn't entirely unexpected was it, considering who our foeman is."

"And you're telling me that one policeman gave it away, our entire plan?"

"It complicates matters, no doubt," Holmes said, ignoring Lestrade's question.

"And heaven knows this business with that devil

was already more complicated than I liked," Lestrade said, in a hoarse voice.

"You don't seem surprised Holmes," I observed as I sat down myself and stared at my friend.

"When you play chess against an adversary like this Watson, will any move you can possibly make surprise him?"

"I suppose not, not if we were speaking of chess," said I, "for he has seen every possible move a thousand times or more, but we aren't talking about chess."

"Indeed Watson, but it is the same principle."

"I should have made preparations to block the street, for this very possibility..." Lestrade mumbled to himself.

"We should speak to the valet," I said.

"That's right!" Lestrade said, leaping to his feet only to stagger dizzily and return quickly to his seat.

"You've had a shock Inspector," I said calmly, "it's best you remain here."

"There is no need to question the young man Watson. Anything DeGreystoke let slip will most surely be a red herring designed only to thwart our progress. I'm afraid we must regroup."

It appeared he was about to make an additional remark when Lestrade rose and staggered out of the room, obviously still feeling the ill effects of the great shock. At that moment I saw Holmes chuckle to himself.

"What is it?" I declared.

"How many people were in the street?"

"You mean, when the carriage raced off?" I asked, confused.

Holmes simply nodded.

"Not counting the carriage driver, the valet, and that devil...two, two more and was there, yes, another two men. Six!" I said.

"One of the couples was a man and woman and you failed to count the man who caused all the trouble in the first place Watson, come now."

"Yes, a woman and the man crossing the street. Seven then, six men and a woman," I said, less sure of myself.

"You see but you do not observe," he said, shaking his head disappointedly. "Do you not recall the presence of a young boy, perhaps twelve years of age?"

"A boy? Surely not," I announced, returning to the window and looking down upon the now nearly empty street. "I recall no boy."

"Nor would most people Watson, but I assure you most sincerely that he was there and a faster sprinter of that age and over a short distance you will not find in all England."

"Then where did he go?"

"No doubt he was on the back of the carriage when it raced off or soon thereafter."

"He was one of yours?" I exclaimed, "One of the Irregulars."

"Little Hodgkins," Holmes said with a chuckle. "The lad shows promise."

"And neither DeGreystoke nor his driver will be aware of his presence or suspect it. He'll be with them all the way to their destination and then no doubt jump down and blend in with the crowd. Brilliant Holmes," I remarked. "I wish Lestrade could have heard this."

"In his current condition it is perhaps best this way, the less he knows being the better for all. It is a longshot Watson, after all how often does a pawn win the game?"

I'd wondered at Holmes' response to Professor DeGreystoke's startling escape, but hearing the news that Little Hodgkins was still on the case explained it. Sherlock Holmes had long been used to disguising himself as an elderly man and through his employment of the Baker Street Irregulars he made regular use of some of London's youngsters. His theory was that most people didn't consider the oldest or the youngest members of society to be threats equal to those from the great middle mass of fully grown adults, more or less in their prime. This, in his opinion, rendered them nearly invisible and, therefore, of great value to Holmes.

"We can only hope that in this desperate case your pawn can play the winning hand."

We took the Hansom back to Baker Street and

relieved the policeman on duty, only to find Nurse Chadwick ready with her disinfectant.

"Professor Findley is feeling much improved but you Gentlemen must not overtax him."

The woman reminded me of a certain Sergeant-Major I'd known in the 66th Berkshire Regiment of Foot, Tolliver by name."[33] She had the same stiff neck, high-cheekbones, and imperious tone.

"He has escaped then," the little man stated as a fact more than asked as a question. "He plays a challenging game and I told you that he likes to be the one in control.

"Yes, well this time we may yet surprise him," I said. "He got away but one of Holmes' boys was apparently latched on to the back of the man's brougham."

I was pleased to note the look of surprise upon the Professor's face.

"We should know shortly where our adversary has taken himself and Inspector Lestrade has promised to keep his men in readiness. Whatever his next move is we may yet be able to foil him."

"Having seen to it that I contracted this deadly disease and unaware that you knew a specialist in the field Dr. Watson, Professor De Greystoke will feel free to disappear. By the way," said he, "I am much indebted to you for my life, for I don't doubt that there are still a great many men in this country whose remedy would have been to bleed me dry with leaches."

---

[33] "The 66th Berkshire Regiment of Foot (Infantry)", by J. Percy Groves, pub. in London by Hamilton, Adams & Co. ©1887.

"No doubt you're correct Professor," I agreed, "for the weight of precedent is a difficult goad to kick against and once a remedy is in place, even if it is of questionable value, it is a chore to displace it."

"I must say that Dr. Stanley and his staff have been a most pleasant surprise Dr. Watson."

I was pleased to hear the man's appreciation and even more happy to see him recovering. The bluish tinge and the wrinkled skin had vanished and a rosy hue now touched his cheeks.

"So you think we're facing the disappearance of Fitzwilliam DeGreystoke now?" I asked him.

He and Holmes exchanged glances to see if they were on the same page, then the little man seemed to speak for them both.

"If Fitzwilliam DeGreystoke had planned to flee the Old Country Dr. Watson, he most assuredly would have sold his substantial properties. Doing so, however, would have sent a signal to anyone watching. It would have told someone like Sherlock Holmes that great changes were in store. This was an advantage Fitzwilliam would have refused to give us. No doubt his hope was to avoid the need to sell out, but despite the deplorable delay in notifying Sherlock, you men acted with such great alacrity that you actually took him by surprise. He countered your move, of course we knew he would, and through several brilliant moves, culminating in his King's Castle, he managed to escape your trap. Sherlock's deductions regarding Grimthorpe again put him in a difficult position, upon his heels so to speak, but now we know that he'd already won the game as far as he was concerned. I was old and he'd infected me with the Cholera bacteria which he no doubt acquired across the Channel in France."

"The continent is struggling with the outbreak even as we speak," said I, "and it would have been simplicity itself to have acquired it."

"No doubt he expected that I would die within a week and in agony at that, and his revenge would be satisfied. While his game hadn't quite gone to plan, he could nonetheless be satisfied with my death, even if it cost him a great deal. Such is the man with whom you are currently engaged."

"So, fully expecting your death, he'll now turn his back on his wealth and flee?" I asked.

"I expect him to flee and while that will be done without the fortune his properties would have merited, I doubt not that he will be most comfortable for the remainder of his life."

"But where?"

"Prussia I would expect, as the place was always a topic of fascination for him. He had a marked fascination for Frederick the Great all the years I knew him and often voiced his praise for Prussia's wars of expansion. I suspect he may have secretly taken up lands there already, as a sanctuary in case matters went against him at any point, not just now. However, as Sherlock has pointed out, none of Fitzwilliam's earlier murders raised suspicion so he was free to continue upon his path both undeterred and undetected."

In the company of Professor Findley I often felt I was with a second Holmes; however, the lethargy of the Oxford Don was a far cry from Holmes' almost canine joy at the cry of, "the game is afoot!"

Even without suffering from the full force of the diabolical infection to which DeGreystoke had subjected him, I suspected that Professor Findley would have been true to his formerly stated word that action "on the ground" was not one of his strengths.

"Tell me honestly Dr. Watson, in your best medical opinion, am I wrong to believe that I can survive this disease? For to tell you the truth Sir, since Dr. Stanley began me upon his radical treatment," he said, gesturing to the upturned bottle of saline solution which hung upon its pole, "I feel that all I require to be right again is but a little sleep."

"I must admit Professor," I answered, "that I am truly happy, even amazed, at your...miraculous recovery. I knew Dr. Stanley had progressed in the treatment of Cholera beyond me and beyond most others even, but I had no idea that his theory of 'oxygenated salts' to augment and restore the vitality of the blood, would have such convincing results."

"Well thank you John," said the man himself, stepping through the door into what Holmes so often referred to as our sanctum sanctorum. "I wish I could get such glowing reports of my treatment from our Old Guard within the Establishment, but alas they remain scandalously conventional and provincial, suspicious of anything that goes beyond their beloved leaches and of bleeding a patient half to death."

"Dr. Stanley," the little Professor exclaimed, "I

will ask you the same question I just now put to Dr. Watson before your arrival. Am I wrong to believe that I can survive this disease?"

"Have you followed my regimen and kept down your food and drink?" Dr. Stanley asked.

"I have and Nurse Chadwick, bless her soul, can attest to it."

"And your nausea, has it tempered somewhat?"

"I feel a new steadiness, I'm thankful to report."

"And your face and hands have filled out and that fateful blue has been replaced with a pleasant rosiness around the cheeks, I see. What of your cramps?"

"A lingering tenderness here and there but no recurrence of the cramping itself."

"I see," said the doctor, sitting and taking pulse and blood pressure. "A good strong regularity there John," said he, looking across at me.

"I found the same upon my return," I replied, smiling.

"You have done well Professor Findley, better than most even. Your outlook is, I would say, guarded but positive. You must not, however, become overly confident in your recovery and then begin behaving in a cavalier manner. Such a thing could easily put you beyond the power of my ability to restore you."

"Cavalier?" repeated the Professor, confused.

"Yes Sir, cavalier, I've seen it too many times, believe me. It is when a patient who is but lingering at Death's Door one minute, confirming the dictates of their last will and testament and preparing for funerary rights, suddenly feels so much better that they forget all their former fears completely. You Sir are fighting a deadly disease which kills most of those she infects and all within mere hours or days and you must not become cavalier, traipsing about the hall or running up and down the stair. Above all do not let me find you dancing down the street!"

"I pledge myself to a sober seriousness Doctor and I disavow all frivolity. There will be no traipsing, running to-and-fro, or dancing, as Nurse Chadwick is my witness."

"In that case," Dr. Stanley said, "I am pleased with your progress, but we must not be surprised with setbacks or some reoccurrence of your former symptoms. My treatment is not magic and Cholera is a powerful enemy once it takes root in the body. While my method achieves better results than the conventional remedies it is not a universal patent for survival."

I recognized the usual cautionary notes in my old classmate's speech but was encouraged by all the positives.

"And despite what the good Dr. Watson might say Professor Findley, I can hardly lay claim to this treatment. I but stand upon the shoulders of others, visionaries like Thomas Latta and John Snow, who went before me and performed the heavy lifting."[34]

---

[34] Dr. Thomas Latta used his intravenous theory during the cholera epidemic of 1832. At the Edinburgh Cholera Hospital he was the first to introduce a saline solution directly into the blood with excellent results. Dr. John Snow worked through the cholera epidemics in London in 1848-49 and again in 1854,

"I cannot thank you and your nurses enough."

"As for the man who did this to you..." Dr. Stanley paused, "well, it is just as well that I am no longer a young man in the full vigor of life, for in all my years I have never heard of another case so black as yours. That anyone alive was capable of imagining, planning, and conducting such a...well, it is a thing I simply cannot believe. I have written a very harsh letter describing this disturbing event to her Majesty's former Chief Medical Officer, Sir John Simon, a man I trust. He will know what to do with the guilty party."

---

successfully disproving the "bad air" or miasma theory of transmission. By mapping cholera cases he proved that it was a water-borne infection originating from a contaminated water supply.

Chapter 10 – Lincolnshire Wheat

"Did you hear the bell Watson?" Holmes asked, later that evening.

He'd been as nervous as a cat as each subsequent hour passed without the expected appearance of the boy he'd dispatched to run DeGreystoke to ground, Little Hodgkins.

"No bell," I replied, "but I heard the door."

Holmes was on his feet immediately and dashed around as fast as feet could fly. I rose in response and turned to face the door.

The Oxford Don

"No bell and no Billy," Holmes muttered.

When we realized that Professor Findley would be with us for the duration of his treatment, I had surrendered my bedroom to him and he was now in there, asleep.

The door opened slowly and through the crack I could see the face before Holmes did.

"It's DeGreystoke," I fairly screamed.

Holmes jerked the door open so quickly that the devil nearly fell into the room.

"Gentlemen, Gentlemen," he said, grabbing the doorframe to keep himself upright. "A little dignity, please."

As he spoke these smooth words his little eyes were darting around the room taking everything in.

"I half expected to find my old companion here, sharing your company," said he, "but he will be too ill for that, no doubt."

"There are just the two of us," Holmes said easily, as if DeGreystoke visited regularly, "as you can see for yourself."

"Of course Mr. Holmes, of course, he is in the next room is he not, dying an ugly, low death? But I would have thought you beyond these childish efforts to deceive me by now, seeing that they never work."

Holmes eyes widened at this comment but he said nothing.

"First there was that tired disguise you used upon the Cirencester train, how long did that take me to see through? All of five minutes, perhaps."

"It was substantially longer than that as I recall,"

I replied indignantly.

"Ah yes, the good Doctor. You never fail do you? You take your natural position so deftly, like a dog in that are you not, always ready to defend your master. Yes, the great detective."

On the train the repulsive little man had called my stories purely fictional accounts meant only to boost my friend's fame, and I wondered now if he truly believed what he'd said. If it had been merely his way of insulting me, I knew he was in for a surprise. Holmes had quietly removed the rattan cane from the bin, the one which housed a secret sword, and my friend was a far better swordsman even than I had hinted at in my stories.

In a flash Holmes had unsheathed the shining silver blade and backed the little man up against our door, keeping the blade at the devil's throat the entire time.

"What now DeGreystoke?" said he, with relish.

"Let us not be boorish Mr. Holmes, for even you cannot be so obtuse as to fail to realize that I would not have entered your lair without an impenetrable shield to protect me. After all, you must admit that I have no Dr. Watson to defend me."

Holmes stared at the man as a glowing light of understanding came into his eyes and he lowered the sword. I wondered what my friend was doing.

"You've gone and misplaced a little waif, have you not? A bad habit that, what, but just as with your tired disguises, I would not be fooled either by you or the child. Can you really be so imprudent as to allow your biographer to supply the whole world

The Oxford Don

with all of your secrets? Poor Mr. Sherlock Holmes, you are so transparent, so terribly transparent aren't you? And especially to me."

"He was not so transparent when he defeated you in that chess game and played you to a stalemate in the very next!" I exclaimed proudly, but I noticed immediately that Holmes grimaced at my words as if he'd been struck actual blows.

DeGreystoke looked at me with those piercing eyes for a long time and then very slowly turned to stare at Holmes.

"That nobody was you?" said he, "That explains so much doesn't it, but then we both know what your good biographer does not, don't we? The events of that night were the result of distraction and luck and a little too much wine."

"You must hope it so DeGreystoke," Holmes remarked, "for if not then the great champion was matched move-for-move by an untried, unproven student barely beyond his youth."

The two staunch adversaries glared at each other in silence as I looked on.

"I have the boy," DeGreystoke said flatly. "He is my safe passage in and out of your demesne."[35]

"And when we let you go, you'll turn him loose, unharmed?" I challenged. "And you accept us to trust you?"

"Look out the window Dr. Watson and tell me what you see," the man said, a disturbing calmness in his threatening voice.

---

[35] Demesne – domain, land, estate.

"It is Hodgkins," I announced. "He's being held by a rough across the street, under the streetlamp, and DeGreystoke's carriage is at the door."

"You need not sound quite so disappointed Dr. Watson, for surely by now you must understand that it is I who am in control here. When will you Gentlemen finally learn that you have no control here whatsoever. You, like the child across the street, are mere pawns in a life-and-death game being played out between me and my old dying friend, Findley. Did you know his family were poor as church mice, living as best they could on some barren rock in the Scottish Sea? The animals spent the cold nights with them in their little hovel and I, Fitzwilliam DeGreystoke, was forced to compete against such a...creature. You can protect him from me just a little longer Gentlemen and then I will read of his death in the Times. All of your efforts to stop me are so sadly in vain. Professor Findley will die just as surely as my elder brother died. Just as my two cousins and all those others died."

"All those others?" I exclaimed.

"Yes Doctor, I'm afraid it is all so very upsetting to your genteel sensibilities, but whether they were great or small, they had to make room for me. I must have my room you see. There's an undeniable destiny in that."

I couldn't believe the words that were coming out of the man before me, and how we were once again helpless to collar him. People often spoke of the devil, but in this man's presence I was left with no doubt at all that evil, however you might be inclined to define it, existed.

"Just as you men will die and in the very act make room for me, you will prove Nietzsche's words true, that the future belongs not to the meek, but to those who will take it."[36]

"You're mad," I said, angrily, "look at yourself!"

"It was inevitable you would see it that way, Dr. Watson. It was as inevitable as your death is, I'm afraid. You are helplessly overmatched and yet you can't allow yourselves to admit it, even when you realize the truth of it. You are already beaten, Mr. Holmes, and if you truly don't see that then you are blinded by pride. Yes, by pride...and naivety."

While Holmes remained silent I spoke again.

"Those words apply to you Mr. DeGreystoke! It is you who are already beaten and too proud to admit it. Only a man as deluded as you could ever look into a mirror and see something superior. The rest of us see nothing but a devil, all twisted and grotesque."

Up to this point he'd been immune to everything I'd said. He was immune to it all. When I spoke next, however, all that changed.

"You're like those grotesque little gargoyles one finds upon the great cathedrals and at the church of the Knights Templar at Rosslyn."[37]

Whatever it was in these words it was like the waving the blanket at the bull. DeGreystoke's hand flashed into his jacket and just as quickly Holmes' blade pressed into the little man's neck.

---

[36] "Thus Spoke Zarathustra," by Friedrich Nietzsche, 1883.
[37] Rosslyn Chapel, Roslin, Midlothian, Scotland.

"There, there," Holmes said, "lay it down slowly upon the little table, just there. That's it, slowly now or I may do something which you will regret."

Professor DeGreystoke removed a pistol from an inside pocket and laid it down.

It was an exquisitely engraved silver .32 caliber pocket revolver, but my mind could only think that DeGreystoke had intended to put at least one of its bullets into me. The man scowled from Holmes to me and back again.

"Take up the pistol Watson and cover our guest from the window. I'll see him down the stairs and if they don't release Hodgkins don't hesitate to fire as many rounds as you can into Mr. DeGreystoke."

Everything went off as Holmes had foreseen and after we saw to Hodgkins and he'd departed, no worse for wear and eager to share the story of his adventure with his mates, I shook my head in amazement.

"How does that fiend continually best us?" I mused.

"He is a chess master after all Watson, practiced in considering any number of moves and counter moves before he commits to the best one available."

"That is certainly a part of it," I agreed.

"Are you suggesting the possibility of something more...supernatural, perhaps?" Holmes asked.

"We are both men of science," I said.

"Then what are you driving at Watson?"

"Only that this devil seems to get the better of us every time."

"And yet," Holmes replied, "we found him out from Professor Findley's scrawled message, chased them out of their hideout in Cirencester, confronted them on the train, discovered them at Grimthorpe, took our man back, and captured his gang in toto, so perhaps the game has gone both ways."

I saw Holmes' point and there was no arguing against its correctness, but to say that I hadn't been bothered by the devil would have been a lie.

"I guess we've given as good as we've gotten," I admitted, finally.

"You drew him out well," Holmes remarked, as we took our seats again.

"Was that what you were wanting, for I confess your silence was unnerving to say the least."

"Yes, it allowed me to observe the man more freely than would otherwise have been possible."

"So do you know where he is, or what?"

Holmes pulled a paper from his pocket and handed it over.

"What do you make of that Watson?"

"Of what? What is this?" I said, staring down at a smudge of pale-yellow powder. "This isn't dirt," I commented, as I sniffed at the sample.

"Not dirt," said he, "but grain. I took it from the mat where he wiped his feet when he entered."

"Grain?" I repeated.

"Lincolnshire wheat to be exact."

I never ceased to be amazed at my friend but that he could really tell where grain originated from was almost too much, even for me.

"Then DeGreystoke is hiding at the Goods Yard at Kings Cross? Not two miles from here. For that is where the wheat is brought in, is it not?" I asked.

"The Granary Building to be more exact," said he, a faint smile playing about his open face. "Although which floor is another question."

"That is incredible," I replied. "Here I thought we'd lost him and yet, from the least likely detail you deduce the location of this blackguard down to a single building in London."

"To be honest Watson, it is rather a large one."

"And what of Lestrade?"

"I sent Billy off with a message before I came back upstairs," he admitted. "The Police will ring the Goods Yard at 2 AM making sure to place men in the four tunnel tubes running beneath the building."

"So unless DeGreystoke has learned to fly, we finally have him," I declared, elated at the thought.

"These are your instructions, my dear Watson, and you must follow them to the letter for I need not remind you of the back-and-forth game we've been playing with one of the most brilliant devils on this earth. If he can think of a way to evade you, he will."

I looked my instructions over and saw that I'd be given four men to search the first two of six levels. Others would monitor the exits, stairwells, and elevators, but it was our duty to clear the level, insuring that DeGreystoke was not there.

"It seems straightforward enough," said I, "I will take the center aisle with two men on both my left and right. We will proceed with one man from each side walking to me in the center and then the three of us move one row forward. Only after we've gotten to the next aisle do the outliers move forward. Then the two men with me walk to the outliers. We continue this overlapping inspection of the two lower floors and then meet in the front of the building. Lestrade and his men have the third and fourth levels and you and your team have the fifth and sixth levels as well as the roof. Afterward, if nothing is found, we'll form two teams and check the transit sheds."

"Precisely Watson," Holmes said, "and vigilance is our watchword."

"How was it that you deduced his location from so little a bit of the grain as was on the rug?" I asked.

"You know my methods well Watson. The vital importance of observing the smallest details cannot be overstated. The bits of grain and germ which were left behind him were little enough to be sure, but so too is the movement of a compass needle and if a man is diligent and focused he may follow it to the North Pole. I knew there was one central Granary nearby and it managed, almost without exception, the wheat of Lincolnshire. As you may know from my monograph on the subject, the wheat from that area is among the palest of golden hues in the Kingdom. When I saw the coloration of the remains I was certain where DeGreystoke had picked it up on his shoes. The rest was elementary."

"But does it hold that we'll still find him there?"

"Beyond the obvious facts that he was there at some point after he escaped Curzon Street and discovered the presence of Little Hodgkins, that he then spent time in the transfer of at least some bags of grain, that he wrote a letter of substantial length to someone in the Province of Brandenburg in the Kingdom of Prussia, and that he plans to be some time upon a grain ship bound for the Continent, I can deduce nothing else."

"My dear Holmes!" I exclaimed in wonder. "You continue to perform the most incredible feats imaginable."

"It is all quite elementary," said he, waving aside my words of praise with a philosophical air.

"You say that and you function as if anyone could have done it...and yet it always comes down to Sherlock Holmes."

"That he was himself engaged in moving bags of grain was obvious by the unmistakable fibers which come from the burlap present upon the thighs of his pants, where a bag rubs when it is carried by hand. That he wrote a letter of substantial length could be seen by the fresh ink stain upon his index finger which I noticed when he placed the gun upon the table. The stain was exactly where it would have been had he repeatedly dipped too deeply into the bottle. That the letter was going to someone in the Province of Brandenburg was clearly written upon the envelope which was exposed when he reached for his gun."

"And his plans to be some time upon a grain ship bound for the Continent," I asked.

"It is quite obvious my dear fellow," said he, "for why else would Fitzwilliam DeGreystoke be moving bags of grain, if not to build a hiding place for himself in the center of a pallet of grain? And why hide in a such a place if it is only going to be distributed to London's bakers? No, each week a grain ship sets sail from the Custom House next to the Billingsgate Market, for the Port of Calais. It therefore holds that our adversary plans to see himself clear of our fair city without the slightest difficulty."

"It's a brilliant plan," I stuttered, stunned at the thought of it, "He'd be invisible."

"And that is why Lestrade is bringing a bundle of sharpened iron rods which will be used to pierce the bags staged for shipment in the transit sheds."

"The man will have to show himself or risk being run through."

"And as the pallets are staged in a long line for loading your four men must pierce both the front and back simultaneously."

"So two in the back and two in the front and proceed the full length of the line."

"Just so Watson. That should force our man to call it quits."

"It is a frightening prospect to be run through by an iron skewer," I grimaced. "By the way, when does the loading begin?"

"Tomorrow morning. So you see he must be in place tonight, unless..."

The Oxford Don

Chapter 11 – Move Against Move

"Unless what?" I demanded, overcome by my curiosity.

"My dear Watson, I must give you something?" said he, and with this he rose and went saying something to himself which, try as I might, I could not translate.

Was it even in English I wondered after a moment, or Greek? I couldn't make sense of it but in a few minutes he returned, looking quite pleased with himself.

"What must you give me Holmes?" I asked.

"I must give you something," he repeated, "a thing. A thing!" he emphasized.

"Alright, a thing, but for what reason?"

He stood before me now, staring in that puzzling way of his, but said nothing.

"It may be Watson," said he, at last, "that you are not yourself luminous, but that you are a conductor of light. Without possessing genius I cannot help but marvel at your remarkable power to stimulate it in me."

In one form or another I'd heard this more times than I cared to, but tonight was somehow different and I could sense it.

"In recognition of your valuable contributions I very much want you to have this my dear fellow."

With that he drew a red leather case with shining gold trim from behind his back and handed it over.

"But Holmes!" I stammered in disbelief, "that was given to you by…"

"His Holiness never need know."

"But" I continued to stammer, "it was your great reward for solving the case of the..."

"And as such I hope that it will convey my gratitude for your...partnership."

I opened the case and beheld one of the most beautiful items of jewelry I had ever seen. It was a pin of pure gold from the Etruscan Period and was mounted by a magnificent, luminescent pearl. That the Pope had bestowed the priceless piece upon Holmes for solving the abstruse case of the Vatican Poisonings only added to my sense of wonderment.

"But why Holmes?" I finally asked, as he sat down in his chair.

"Why?" he declared, "Why? It is a gesture long overdue, now that I consider it my good fellow, and one which I am pleased to see has touched you."

"Indeed," I agreed wholeheartedly, "but still I'm puzzled."

"You have seen the track I've been following, the line of reasoning which would have led us to the search for DeGreystoke at the Goods Yard."

"Yes and your deductions were brilliant!"

"Just a little too brilliant Watson, I would say."

"Too brilliant? I don't follow."

"Did I not find the clues too easily?" said he, looking down into his cup. "Was not the smudge of grain too obvious upon the mat? The grain dust too thick upon his patent leather shoes? And were not the threads of burlap just a bit too visible upon the black pants? And would the man who despises

Professor Findley for his humble origins ever lift a bag of grain for himself, let alone dozens?"

"But the Granary Building is not two miles..."

"And wouldn't he have been aware that I would be reading every clue? What did he say? That we must understand he was the one in control, not us."

"Yes, that we were like little Hodgkins, merely pawns in his game against Professor Findley."

"So every clue he showed me was something he wanted and expected me to see...and react to, and what have I done?"

"You've deduced his plan!"

"I, who trusts in observation, was so easily misled by my observations. As he mocked me earlier in this very room, calling me a fool for allowing you print all my methods for the whole world, including DeGreystoke himself, to read. Yes, I have been misled and I've called down a whole host of Policemen to descend upon the Goods Yard in Kings Cross at 2 AM, making sure to place men in the tunnels even. Oh, how DeGreystoke would have loved that. And what was the supreme beauty of his plan Watson, can you guess it?"

"I'm afraid I can't."

"It would have taken us hours to have conducted the search and when we didn't find him..."

"We would have doubted our search and, being cautious, we would have maintained the outer ring and conducted another."

"By which time he would have been in France!"

"What's that?" I cried, "France? But Holmes, the Brandenburg Letter..."

"Yes, the Brandenburg Letter, that was a touch was it not? He is indeed the chess master and but for Sherlock Holmes' 'secret weapon' he would have had me Watson, I assure you he would have."

"A secret weapon? Holmes, I know nothing of this. What is it?"

"Of course you know about it my good fellow," said he, excitedly, "although I can hardly blame you for not thinking of it. It is you Watson! You are my secret weapon."

I was speechless and searched my friend's face to see if he were serious or was this some elaborate jest at my expense.

"Think Watson, Professor Findley told you that many of the most brilliant minds suffer from a debilitating phenomenon."

"Yes," I said, "they underestimate those around them."

"Habitually," said a soft voice behind me and when I turned I saw Professor Findley standing there on his own strength and looking quite his old self.

"But what was it you said when I told you about the plan for the Goods Yard?"

I tried to recall but we'd said so much that I was unable to think of what Holmes might be referring to and I shook my head.

"You said and I quote, 'so unless DeGreystoke has learned to fly, we finally have him!' Do you recall that now?"

"Of course," said I, "but that was merely a figure of speech."

"Figure of speech or no, Watson, you possess the remarkable power of stimulating my mind. How did he get the cholera bacteria into England while it was still capable of causing infection? That is the question."

That the devil DeGreystoke had done what he'd

done to Professor Findley still horrified me and that he was willing to risk another epidemic in our country, with perhaps hundreds of thousands killed, was something my sane mind couldn't fathom.

"Are you saying that he flew?" I asked.

"As you said Dr. Watson," Professor Findley replied, "unless DeGreystoke has learned to fly, we finally have him. Well Sir, I'd say he learned to fly."

"Indeed," Holmes agreed, "once we eliminate the impossible whatever remains, even if it is highly improbable, will be the truth. DeGreystoke has learned to fly and do you recall where the aeronaut, Richard Scott Coxswain, made his ascents?"[38]

"Cremorne Pleasure Gardens, I recall it was a spectacular sight."

"And in the opposite direction from the Granary at Kings Cross."

"It is," I declared, in surprise. "It seems he thought of everything."

"He thought of everything but you Watson. You he underestimated and now, if we are quick, we can take him red handed."

"What can I do?" I asked.

"Go to Scotland Yard and inform Lestrade of the change. Then, as quickly as you can, come to Cremorne. Unless you can see the balloon, start in

---

[38] Henry Tracey Coxwell – The Illustrated London News declared him the foremost English balloonist of the last half of the Nineteenth Century. He flew in England and the Continent, led two companies of balloonists in the Franco-Prussian War (1870), and supplied one balloon to the British Army in the Third Anglo-Ashanti War.

the large field by Ashburnham Hall. I'll go there directly and if I see nothing I'll begin at the Garden Circle. Hopefully we can collar this killer before the sun rises."

"I would go with you," Professor Findley said to Holmes.

I was about to remonstrate with the man and give him my best medical recommendation but Holmes held up his hand.

"It is no use Watson," said he. "When he makes his decisions there is no power in heaven or on earth which can dissuade him, and that includes the Dean of Christ Church College, Oxford."

"Just ask my wife Doctor, she can give you her attestation that Sherlock is quite correct."

We all prepared quickly for our departure and there was no mistaking Holmes' excitement. The game, at last, was truly afoot and it was at moments like this he was most like a bloodhound, eager to be away. When I reached Scotland Yard at half eleven, Inspector Lestrade was already hunched over a giant map of London with his officers.

"I'm afraid there is a change of venue Inspector," said I, interrupting their planning.

"The devil you say Dr. Watson, I've already set the outer ring and we were just about to..."

"I'm very sorry," I said, interrupting him again, "but Mr. Holmes believes Cremorne Gardens is now the sight of DeGreystoke's escape."

"Cremorne Gardens? I've never heard anything so preposterous in all my life, the pleasure gardens and amusement park. You couldn't make this up in

The Oxford Don

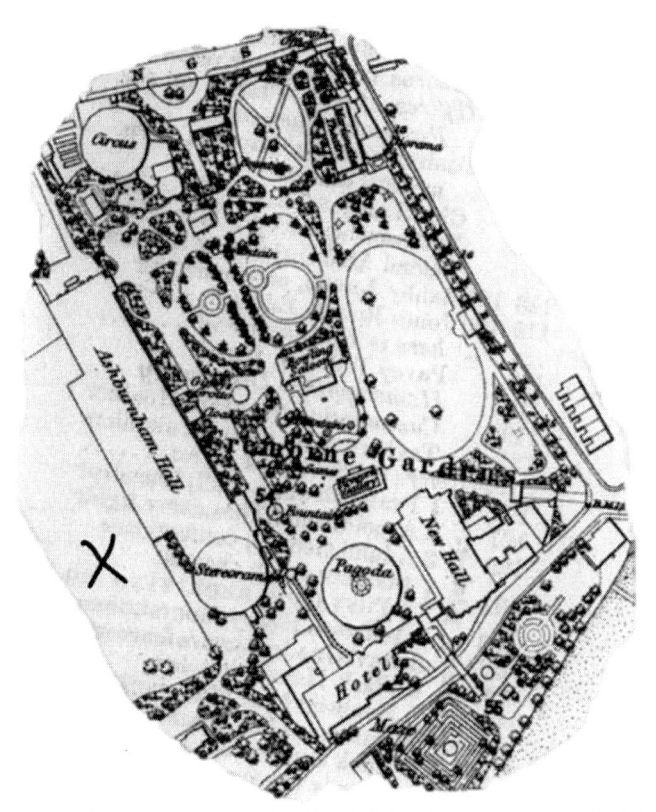

one of your stories Sir," said he in understandable consternation.

"I'm afraid it is so, nonetheless."

"Well, perhaps it is Dr. Watson, but I'm putting half my men at the Goods Yard anyway, just as a precaution. I will not have it said that Inspector Lestrade let down his guard this time. The rest of us will come wherever you lead and we'll see which place proves right."

It happened very much as the Inspector had ordered and a short time later a half dozen Police

Carriages came to a stop along the Ashburnham Hall field, only to see the dark silhouette of a giant balloon rising into the dark night sky. I ran as fast as I could, finally throwing my cane aside to gain what little extra speed I could. Several of the young men in uniform outpaced me, but it was no use. The balloon was away and the only light was a ring of lanterns DeGreystoke and his pilot had used to prepare the balloon. I could see the little man, his expression twisted in a rare delight, shaking his fist into the air.

"You are too late you meddlers! Too late Mr. Sherlock Holmes. You've been beaten."

We all stood and stared. I was yet again in a state of incredulity that we had been bested by the devil I'd come to know as DeGreystoke. The officers and the lean faced Lestrade stared as the man continued to shake his fist bitterly in the air in the fading reflections of the lanterns. Even Holmes and Professor Findley, when they came up, continued to stare hopelessly.

"The wind is out of the northwest at a 2 to 3 on the Beaufort Wind Force Scale," Professor Findley said quietly to Holmes as he stared at the flag atop the Cremorne Gardens Hotel.[39]

"It's a Sidcup-Swanley-Staplehurst-New Romney line of flight then," Holmes muttered almost to himself without taking his eyes from the quickly fading balloon.

---

[39] The Beaufort Scale was named for Rear Admiral Sir Francis Beaufort and was made the standard for Royal Naval vessels in the late 1830's.

"With a landing in the Boulogne-Sur-Mer area of France I calculate," our Oxford Don said, then he added, "if unimpeded."

At that moment Holmes withdrew Professor DeGreystoke's engraved silver pocket revolver and pointed it skyward.

The little revolver called out four shots in quick succession, then Holmes returned it fittingly to his pocket.

"Your attempts are pointless Mr. Holmes," that by now familiar voice hollered back from the sky.

"I'm afraid he's right," Lestrade said, his smile shining golden in the lantern light. "You'll never bring that monster down with a bullet."

"A bullet might not bring it down Inspector," Professor Findley replied, "but it would take a greater fool than Fitzwilliam DeGreystoke to risk a crossing of the English Channel in a balloon so damaged."

"The tragic deaths of the French Aeronauts, deRozier and Romain, sadly come to mind Inspector," Holmes added, "and they began their crossing from Boulogne-Sur-Mer in a perfectly fit balloon as I recall."[40]

My friend inevitably phrased many of his statements with "as I recall," in the attempt to sound less sure of virtually every topic he addressed. This isn't to say he knew a great deal about every subject, for he was scandalously ignorant of broad swaths in a great many topics. However, he was famously knowledgeable upon those topics he usually chose to address.

"So they'll have to put down to see to repairs," I exclaimed, thrilled at the realization that we might still have a chance to apprehend our adversary.

"Yes Watson," Holmes replied calmly, "and they'll have to put down upon on a Sidcup-Swanley-Staplehurst-New Romney line."

"I'm sorry to tell you Mr. Holmes, but we'll never catch them with the horses."

"Not in the long-run Inspector Lestrade," the Professor offered, "but in the shorter distance the horses may outpace the balloons to a surprising degree, especially as the streets at this time of night

---

[40] Pilatre de Rozier and Pierre Romain died in their 1785 attempt to cross the English Channel.

are nearly empty and the clouds, behold, begin to open for the moon."

"You are correct however, Inspector Lestrade, that our greatest hope must lie in your message to activate the constabularies along that line of travel."

"That and the fact that the landing, repairs, and subsequent relaunching of the monster, as you call it, will be impossible to achieve before morning."

Lestrade stared as the meaning of all of these words slowly dawned upon him.

"Then I must notify them," he cried suddenly, "and you Gentleman may take one of the carriages to follow as you will." As the man sprinted off the field followed by his confused men, he screamed back over his shoulder that he would send messages to Sidcup and then farther down the line to keep us updated.

"We'll beat the balloon to Sidcup at least," Holmes called out as we trotted toward our carriage.

"We can take the night train from just beyond there, in Swanley, if we fall behind," the breathless Oxford Don said, as he climbed into the carriage.

His knowledge of the train schedules, even in districts far removed from his world of Oxford, was clearly akin to Holmes' encyclopedic knowledge of the subject.

"For a man who was only recently at death's door Professor, you are doing surprisingly well," I said, "but I must warn you that when Dr. Stanley hears of your escapades you will find matters exceedingly warm."

"If Dr. Watson, say rather, if," said he with a glint in his eyes which spoke volumes.

We raced through Battersea at a steady trot, across Clapham Commons, through West Dulwich and into Sydenham, the distance of a few miles but our horses were quite spent. While our police driver changed horses with the help of the officer on duty at the Sydenham Constabulary we scanned the sky.

"There it is," Holmes said, pointing back toward London.

"And only at about 1,500 feet," I said.

"They are staying low for a reason Doctor," the Professor said, ominously. "If the fabric rips they will need to put down quickly, wherever they are, or face the alternative."

The "alternative" the little man had alluded to was obviously a painful death in the latest ballooning accident in England.

The thing was by turns silhouetted against the clouds or illuminated by the moon and was difficult to keep track of, especially in the vicinity of the streetlamps. In the open country we had a better chance of keeping track of it.

"I'd say we're two miles ahead of it right now," Holmes said, as the carriage got underway with two fresh horses.

"Three miles to Sidcup," I said, "more or less, and that again to Swanley, then West Kingsdown, and again to Wrotham Heath. That's the track you spoke of Holmes."

"Indeed, but we'll need to change horses again at Swanley if we're to keep up with them."

"Can they know we're ahead of them?" I asked.

"No doubt Fitzwilliam has been tracking our progress with a glass, much as we are watching them," Professor Findley replied, shocking me. "For from such a low elevation our carriage lamps would make us quite obvious upon the roads."

"So it really is a case of check and checkmate," I declared. "As long as we can change out our horses they dare not descend, but there is only so much of England left and it is rapidly lessening."

At Sidcup Holmes retrieved three telegrams from Inspector Lestrade. The first simply said that all the posts along the line had been notified and men were being called in to watch for the balloon. The second said that he'd commissioned the Police Engine and would soon be on the rails behind us. The third informed us that they were at Eltham and were directly beneath the balloon.

"At this rate we'll reach Swanley at the same time as the engine," Holmes remarked, "and we'll still have a lead on the balloon."

"And should we transfer to the train?"

"To do so would be to put all of our proverbial eggs into the one basket Dr. Watson," Professor Findley noted, "and it would tie us solely to the line of the track."

"As long as the carriage can keep up we are better deployed here," Holmes added, "and should they descend they will find we've preempted them."

"Yes, I hate to think of such a man escaping us again."

"It is as you've said Doctor, a game of move against move and as you are pitted against one of the greatest chess masters of all time, you must not allow yourself to imagine that he has not been thinking several ahead."

The words had a chilling effect upon me for in them I suddenly realized the very means Fitzwilliam DeGreystoke would use to slip through our fingers once again.

"Holmes," I hissed desperately, as I knocked upon the roof of the carriage to stop it. I scrambled out and pointed skyward. "Look!"

"It has increased its elevation," Holmes noted.

"Very odd," Professor Findley mused.

"Not at all odd if he plans to use a parachute," I proclaimed confidently.[41]

"Have they really advanced so far?" the little man asked, the topic clearly being a field beyond his usually reckoning.

"They have!" said I, emphatically, "and I assure you Gentlemen, the devil means to jump for it. With the repairs being so laborious and the area to land in decreasing rapidly he will not risk it. He will jump."

Holmes pointed upward at that moment and there, where the moonlight was streaming through a break in the clouds, the balloon and its basket were suddenly illuminated in a bright, shifting radiance.

"I do believe the man means to jump for it Watson," said he, in obvious surprise.

We stood next to the carriage and watched in silence. Even our driver, a young Irishman named Kelly, stared in wonder at the sight of the little form sitting high above us along the rim of the basket, the legs, illuminated for but a moment in the rays of moonlight, dangling in midair.

"This is incredible," I said to Holmes, for even though I knew of the advances in the field I had never seen a man jump from so great a height.

"What is to be done Sherlock?" the Professor asked, with an odd uncertainty in his voice.

---

[41] American Balloonist John W. Wise made over 400 flights and was responsible for countless improvements to balloon design, ballooning techniques, and parachutes. On September 18, 1837, he dropped two inverted parachutes of the modern type, with good results.

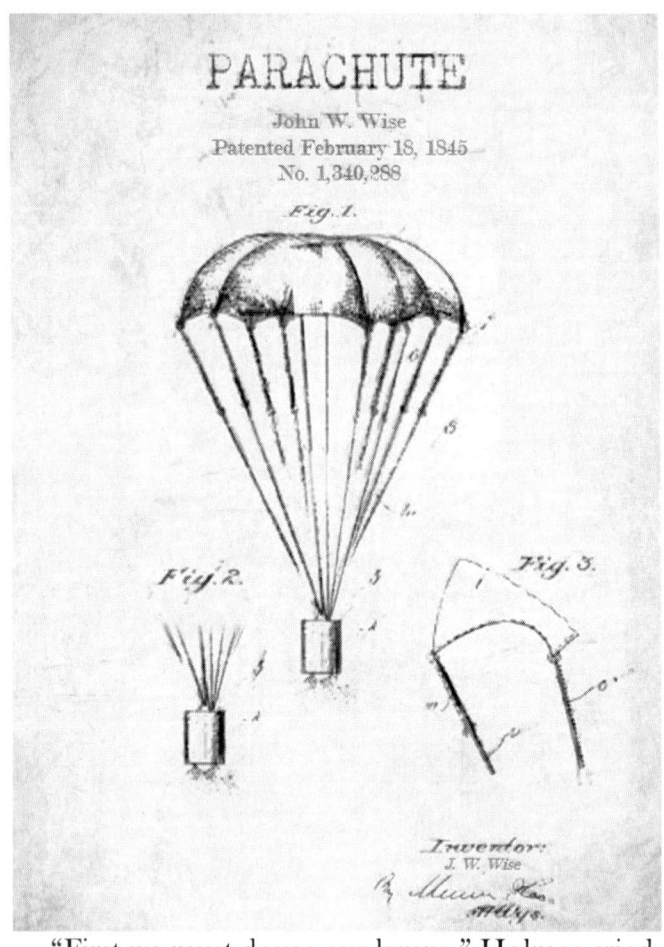

> PARACHUTE
> John W. Wise
> Patented February 18, 1845
> No. 1,340,288
>
> Fig. 1.
>
> Fig. 2.   Fig. 3.
>
> Inventor:
> J. W. Wise

"First we must douse our lamps," Holmes cried, "and then we must pursue him," Holmes replied. "He knows we must pursue him but we cannot let him track us as easily as we have."

"Then he has already arranged for someone to be where near, surely, for although it was purely an insurance against just such a disaster he would not have left such a thing to chance."

The Professor's words reminded us that all of this was a great life-and-death game to DeGreystoke and we were immediately mobilized. Instead of staring at the balloon, we four now went to searching the fields far below the high plateau of the North Downs where we had stopped.

"There!" shouted Constable Kelly, pointing due south along the Darent River and a mile west of Wrotham Village.

Every eye turned to see the glowing lamps of a brougham carriage with two horses, not more than a mile distant in a straight line, but far below in the valley and perhaps three miles away as the roads wended around.

"Can you get us there Constable, to that spot?" Holmes asked, for the terrain was steep and the roads outside the village were few.

"Just watch me Mr. Holmes," the man said, thrilled to have the chance to prove himself at last.

"I must admit Gentlemen, that it is quite exciting to share one of your adventures," Professor Findley admitted when we regained our seats.

Holmes nodded and braced one foot against my seat opposite as our carriage began to careen down the steep road that rolled away southeast toward Wrotham Village and down into the valley, and all in nothing but the shifting moonlight.

I kept the balloon in sight as much as I could until we finally reached the bottom of great scarp and leveled off into the valley.

"There, there!" I shouted. "He's done it!"

My companions strained now to see what I was

seeing, the amazingly bright illumination of a great mushroom shape which seemed suspended in the night sky.

"I never dreamed of such a thing," the Professor admitted in a whisper. "To think Fitzwilliam, who was terrified to go above the first rung of a ladder, has jumped from a balloon at several thousand feet. What is our world coming to?"

"I'm afraid that evil awakens a malignant kind of genius Professor and promotes a great many deeds which would never have been undertaken. Among these unfortunately are some of the most malicious imaginable. In a mind like Mr. DeGreystoke's, the possibilities must be considered almost...limitless."

Even in the dim light I could see a deep sadness writ broad across Holmes' expression. It brought his words back to my mind, that there were some trees which grew to a set height quite normally then, apparently without any cause or reason whatsoever, developed some unsightly eccentricity.

While men like Lestrade and me could only see the twisted, black nature in DeGreystoke, and men like Professor Findley could only recall their good memories, Holmes could see more. In his mind I imagined visions of what good such a man as Fitzwilliam DeGreystoke might have done had evil not mastered the man first.

"I think they've seen us," I said, pointing at the brougham, "for they are on the move."

"No," Holmes mumbled distractedly, "they're moving not so much to avoid us Watson, as to be nearer the place of DeGreystoke's landing."

I watched and could see that Holmes was correct, they had not seen us and with our lamps out we were merely another dark spot in a dark night.

"Your realization regarding the parachute was quite brilliant Watson," Holmes remarked, as he kept his eyes upon DeGreystoke.

"Indeed it was Doctor," the Oxford Don agreed, "for without that we might otherwise have missed his desertion of the balloon altogether and even now found ourselves miles from here."

I was pleased to hear the praises of two such men, but especially from Holmes. We could all see the parachute now without the need to crane our necks.

"It draws nearer the earth," the Professor noted quietly.

"At about a thousand feet now, I'd estimate," I offered, "and its movement is more discernible."

"He will be stiff and cold when he alights and the fields are wet, as we know from the landlord of the Plough in Stalisfield Green."

"I wish we could have communicated the man's jump to Lestrade," I admitted.

"He may still have seen the parachute Watson, even if they weren't expecting it. He has a good many eyes with him upon the train and instead of racing to get somewhere, they're tracking the progress of the balloon in as close a proximity as the rails allow.

Constable Kelly turned north to follow the other carriage along the narrow road that followed the Darent River westward toward its headwaters. In the meantime the rays of the moon illuminated the canopy of the inverted parachute, as they were called, and made it glow in an eerie brightness.

"He's nearly down," I pointed out, "just a few hundred feet more and he'll be in that field."

Constable Kelly saw that our horses were pushed to a faster pace to close the gap with the leading carriage.

"Now there's no telling who or how many will be there," Holmes pointed out.

"Or how great a fight they'll give us," I said, "but I have my revolver."

"And I have DeGreystoke's pocket revolver," Holmes said, "but with just one bullet remaining."

"Surely Gentlemen, we can resolve this without resorting to violence," Professor Findley declared.

"It is a romantic notion," Holmes replied, "and I well recall your views on violence Professor. It may be that the threat of using it will be enough alone to quell our opponents, but if not..."

"I shudder to think this will end in bloodshed Sherlock and I pray you will exhaust every other avenue..."

"I'm afraid that...on the ground, we have to move too quickly for that," Holmes said honestly, "but you insisted on accompanying us and you must stay the course now that you've begun it. I don't expect you to join in but by the same token you must promise not to interfere with us." After a long pause Holmes added, "I'd hate to have to inform Queenie that having saved you from the villain we lost you to his henchmen in the final battle.

Chapter 12 – Checkmate

Once we'd arrived Constable Kelly set the brake and followed as Holmes and I walked up either side of the carriage. I ordered the lone man in the cab and the driver out and down a gun point and put them on their knees on the road. Even as I did the shadow of DeGreystoke came down in the center of the boggy.

"Constable," Holmes said as he handed the young man the silver revolver, "if they move..."

"I understand Sir," he replied, "you can count on me."

"Watson you take a line to the right and I'll take the left, we must not allow DeGreystoke to doubleback upon us and get through to the road."

I jumped the ditch half filled with water from the recent rains and climbed a rough wooden gate. When I jumped down I sank several inches into the sodden ground and realized that was the sound I'd heard when our adversary landed. Without waiting I took off at a jog across the black field hoping there were no hidden obstacles in the field. I noticed Holmes' lean form fifty feet to the left but had yet to see DeGreystoke. I even had trouble making out the parachute now that it was down and no longer glowed with the moonlight. Holmes called out more than once to find my location and when we reached the spot from which our bird had flown I imagined all manner of diabolical escapes.

"He's not here!" I cried. "I can see nothing."

"He's making for the far corner," Holmes said, grabbing my left forearm, "can you see him, just there?"

I saw nothing then looked again.

"I see him."

"We must get him Watson."

For the first time I could hear the desperation in my friend's voice. He had maintained a calm mask in the face of our setbacks but I could tell that the tension of every setback had weighed on him.

"If he escapes us now Watson, we may not have another chance."

My nerves were fairly shot too but I put all my strength into sprinting across the water-logged field. I found that the sound of DeGreystoke's running and breathing were my greatest aids and soon closed in on the little man. He was in the corner, penned in on one side by a patchwork of a wooden fence, and on the other by a rickety wooden gate tied shut with a length of rope. I could see him clearly now as I approached and he took to darting this way and that in order to avoid his final capture. He reminded me of the rat who suddenly finds himself cornered by the even fiercer terrier, ready to set upon him. The buzzing hum of my silver-headed cane as I swung it round and round soon convinced the little man that his only path to safety lay over the fence.

With a great effort he freed himself from the mud and nearly made it over the top before I laid my hands upon him. I pulled him back with such force that he slammed backward into the deep mud around the gate and slid on his back for several feet before he came to a stop against the legs of Sherlock Holmes. The devil was exhausted and in far worse condition than I would have imagined. He simply lay there gasping for air, his arms oddly akimbo, his legs askew, his eyes bulging out of their sockets, and his tongue lolling to one side. I drew up and took him by the collar of his coat for the second time in the course of the case, the other being in the brake van of the Cirencester Train.

"I've got him now," said I, with deep satisfaction.

"Well done Watson."

"Unhand me you Scythian!" he screamed, just as he had on the train. I continued to hold him firmly by the collar and dragged him through the mud all the way to the gate.

"You knave," he shouted between gulps of air. "You brute!"

"Dr. Watson is that you?" a voice called from the darkness.

"We are here Inspector," I called out, "and we have your man."

DeGreystoke wriggled and wrestled helplessly in the mud at my feet and still I held him stoutly by his collar.

Suddenly lanterns and the lamps of several police carriages were lit upon the road and the night fairly vanished.

"He was running toward us the whole time and didn't even know it!" Lestrade exclaimed happily. "There's a genius for you." Then he saw Holmes coming up out of the veil of darkness. "Halloa Mr. Holmes, I see you Gentlemen have finally put the collar on the little fellow."

"Indeed we have Inspector," Holmes replied, "but it seems he hasn't given up the fight just yet."

"He looks more like a drowned rat right now," Lestrade noted, holding a lantern down next to DeGreystoke's strained visage as the man continued to struggle. "Stop it," he commanded, "or he may just give you the thrashing you deserve."

With that Fitzwilliam DeGreystoke finally went limp at my feet, covered all about with mud and breathing heavily.

When I looked up I saw host of officers looking upon the scene in wonder. They seemed to realize that they were witnesses to the culmination of one of the greatest battles of good and evil ever.

"You know nothing," DeGreystoke scowled at Holmes and me as one of the officers placed the handcuffs on him.

"I know this much Professor," Lestrade replied, very much enjoying himself, "we have a room for you."

"Imbeciles," DeGreystoke growled as he was lifted and dragged him away to the prison wagon.

"Constable Kelly had two of DeGreystoke's men under guard on far side of the field," I said to Lestrade but he merely shook his thin face at me and pointed.

"What do you suppose he's about now Doctor?" Lestrade asked.

Looking around I saw that Holmes was nowhere to be seen and I followed Lestrade's finger pointing back across the field. I could just make out Holmes' thin figure running to and fro in the field, all around the parachute.

"I hardly know Inspector, but I'm certain it will be something of great importance, even if it that reason escapes us at the moment."

"Well, I'll leave you gentlemen to it and wish you a good night. I'll see to our prisoner and get my men back to London. Perhaps it would be good if I dropped by tomorrow?"

"Or rather, today, seeing it's well past midnight."

By the time I reached Holmes it could no longer be called dark, dim yes, wet and cold no doubt, but no longer truly dark, as the sky in the east was faintly brighter.

"What are you doing here?" I said, coming upon my friend as he seemed to be preoccupied with digging in the mud.

"Looking my dear fellow," said he, "looking fervently."

He had that sleuthhound air about him that he had in his most fevered moments and I suspected that whatever he was looking for was something of immense value.

"Yes indeed," I exclaimed, "but for what are you looking?"

"Ah," he cried, digging in the mud nearly thirty feet from where DeGreystoke had landed in the mud. "Here it is Watson, the key to everything unless I'm very much mistaken!" said he, as he straightened up.

For some minutes he was engaged in wiping the mud off the object until finally I could make out the form two small books bound together tightly with a leather strap.

"Books!" I exclaimed.

"Books!" Holmes repeated, "why is that so odd? Men like DeGreystoke order their lives by books and hope that someday their names will fill them by the page."

"To live on forever I suppose," said I, shaking my head at an idea which was foreign to me. "Well, maybe he'll get his wish now that he's been taken, there is a kind of destiny in that."

"Indeed there is Watson, indeed there is."

By the time we reached the road where our carriage now stood alone, DeGreystoke's carriage and accomplices having already been taken away by Inspector Lestrade's men, our appearance solicited a general horror.

"There is no hurry now Constable," Holmes called out as he removed his jacket, "and we will try not to dirty your carriage overmuch."

With that he placed the jacket, inside out, upon the seat and sat down gingerly. I followed his example and we were soon on the move again.

Several hours later, freshly cleaned and finally presentable, Holmes and I ate our lunch while Dr. Stanley examined Professor Findley upon the settee.

"So no traipsing Professor?" the Doctor asked half-jokingly.

"And no dancing down the street Dr. Stanley, as my friends may testify."

"Well, I will give you one more treatment, but only as a precaution as you seem to have recovered surprisingly well I must say."

"And I may return to my wife and my routine tomorrow then?"

"I see no reason holding you back, as long as you promise to see me immediately if you feel the slightest relapse."

After Dr. Stanley and his nurse departed for the final time Professor Findley thanked us in a most cordial manner for all we'd done for him.

"It is what we do," Holmes replied without any further elaboration.

"It was a remarkable experience," Findley said, "and I am obliged to both of you. Might I hope to read about it in some future story of yours Dr. Watson? Such a thing would be a true treat for our circle, I assure you."

"It is a possibility," I replied, without promising more.

Over my years with Holmes I'd found that every now and again a case came along which was so disturbing to my mind that I required the long passage of time before I was again up to wrestling with the writing of the thing. In the case of "The Oxford Don," I had no question that Professor Findley would be waiting a good long time for his circle to read his name in print.

Holmes seemed to sense my feelings upon the subject but, much to my relief, said nothing.

That evening the bell rang and Inspector Lestrade, looking quite disturbed, was shown in.

"Come in Lestrade," Holmes gave a welcoming call, but noticing the man's fallen features he quickly changed his tune. "What is it man, for you are nothing if not crestfallen."

"It is our man Mr. Holmes."

"DeGreystoke?"

"Indeed, our physician passed judgment within the last hour. He is upon his deathbed."

"Deathbed," I repeated, "from what cause?"

"He believes it was a powerful poison."

"So, it's suicide?" Professor Findley asked.

"I cannot say," Lestrade answered, "for the thing is beyond me. I can make neither heads nor tails of it. The man has a slice upon his neck which is much inflamed, but otherwise he seems unblemished by scratches or marks. Which you must admit is quite strange considering his antics of late."

"Could your surgeon be wrong Inspector," I asked, "for we know the man has been handling the Cholera bacterium recently."

"He knows little enough about Cholera to be sure Doctor, and what he knows is probably in keeping with the old ways, but I'd say he's as sound a man as could be found when it comes to poisons. At least that is my opinion of the man."

"And as to this cut Inspector, can you point out upon your neck where it is?" Holmes asked.

"Just here," the man said, drawing his index finger across the jugular upon the right side of the neck.

The movement was so odd that it brought Holmes' handling of his cane-sword back to my memory, for he had laid the blade just there upon DeGreystoke's neck when the latter visited Baker Street.

Professor Findley had remained silent but he was obviously overwrought by the news that his old friend and would-be murderer was now near to his own death.

"Does this convey anything to our mind Mr. Holmes, which you would like to bring to my attention?"

"No Inspector, I think not. As to poison, if that is what DeGreystoke took, he would have found no great challenge in hiding it upon his person."

"You mean like under his tongue or such?"

"Precisely, or along the outside of the jaw, and simply broke the vial when the time came."

"There were no cuts in the man's mouth or throat. The surgeon made a point of checking on that."

"There might be one more possibility Inspector Lestrade," Professor Findley offered. "As Dr. Watson has so aptly pointed out, we know the man handled the Cholera bacterium quite recently and the symptoms of Arsenic poisoning and Cholera can be...similar."

"Yes, but as I just said, there were no cuts in the man's mouth or throat to point to his consumption of either the poison or the bacteria."

"But there is another, much more subtle way of smuggling a fatal dose into prison with him, if that was his plan."

"He was stripped upon being processed and everything upon him was taken Professor, so where might he have hidden this deadly dosage?"

"Under his fingernails Inspector."

The shock of these words hit Lestrade hard and he turned immediately to me.

"Dr. Watson, is that...is such a thing possible? I mean, how long could, or rather, would the bacteria..."

"It is of course possible Inspector, as far as that goes. While the Cholera bacteria is extremely virulent however, it is not so hardy that it could survive indefinitely under exposed conditions. We know it can survive indefinitely within the host, until death in fact and even after, for a period. It might survive under the fingernails for a time, say twenty-four hours, and if ingested during that period it could prove fatal, but there have been no studies upon this question."

"So he could have ingested it at any time in over the past week and not shown the symptoms until he was in our custody?"

"Symptoms can appear in as little as a few hours up to several days, although why he would want to contract the disease while he still held out a realistic hope of escape remains a question?"

"A good question Watson," Holmes remarked.

"I'm sure I don't know," Lestrade said, "all I know is that, just when I thought we'd solved the mystery, this case has become more bizarre and puzzling to me than ever."

"But why should it be puzzling Inspector? You have taken a man into custody for whom human life is of no more worth than that of swine. Would you really expect such a man to keep himself alive only to gratify his jailors upon the occasion of his execution?"

"I guess not, when you put it that way Mr. Holmes. Although now that I think about it who would choose an agonizing death from either arsenic or cholera instead of the merciful speed of the rope? I know I would not."

"You have pronounced both the question and the answer Inspector Lestrade. You are a sane man and as such you would opt for the rope, but the man you have in that cell, you must understand, is not like you. If a man simply had to await the rope there would be little reason not to, but we know very well that a trial must be endured first. Then, depending upon the case, the man who waited for the rope may find himself not sentenced to death at all. The idea of spending the remainder of his life in prison would be a nightmare for a man like DeGreystoke and doubtlessly he would have done anything to insure against that."

"I see," Lestrade said thoughtfully, "and the only way to guarantee an end to it all would be a poison or the disease we know he had access to."

At this point Holmes rose and took the two books he'd found in the field down from the shelf and handed them to the Inspector.

"The first book is DeGreystoke's account book. You will see that he did in fact sell many of his domestic properties prior to launching his attack upon Professor Findley, only he did so privately and not enough at any one time to raise any alarms. He also acquired several properties across Europe. As to his accounts, they were...extremely healthy."

"And the second book?"

"His private journal, complete with descriptions of his grievances against every victim, their names and titles, dates, the methods used to murder them, the benefits he derived from their deaths, and even summaries of what happened in the aftermath of each murder with regard to the police."

Lestrade glanced quickly through the pages of the second book until he noted a familiar name.

"Sir Eustace Delaval? Baron Delaval? That was murder? That was DeGreystoke?"

"That was," Holmes answered.

"Dr. Anson Etheridge-Hill too? Everyone was convinced that was a tragic accident. Why him?"

"It was tragic, but I'm afraid it was no accident. Dr. Etheridge-Hill had given offense, apparently in public the notes say," Holmes answered.

"So he had to die?"

"Such was the deterioration to DeGreystoke's morality Inspector, that by that point in his criminal career those who offended him...died."

"There are a dozen names here, from all over the country."

"The journal offers a sobering view of a man who had abandoned all that it means to be human. The lives of others were only of any worth in what they could supply Fitzwilliam DeGreystoke. The idea of loyalty, even to his only brother, was meaningless to him if their death could supply him with a means of gain. The concept of fairness too, was a moot point. He and his allies could use whatever means and operate in whatever manner best served him. Meanwhile if a man dared notice or complain, he became guilty of causing offence. This opened the victim to any and all the subsequent consequences DeGreystoke felt were justified. This book, in the hands of the court, would vanquish the sympathy of even the kindest heart. DeGreystoke knew he could never mount a defense if the book was discovered."

"But why keep it Holmes?" I asked.

"He was proud of his achievements Watson. In some very real ways DeGreystoke took far more joy and satisfaction from his many murders than he did from his international victories in chess, with all their prizes, awards, medals, titles, and acclaim. He had prevailed against the authorities again and again and each such victory fueled his next endeavor. This book," Holmes said, pointing to the journal, "is the autobiography of a killer who sees no shame in his actions, only an abiding satisfaction and sense of accomplishment."

"You are describing a sick man Mr. Holmes," the Inspector replied.

"One can hardly argue for the sanity of a man who seeks out a virulent disease in order to infect his fellow man. The Cholera Bacterium kills and it kills en masse. It is nothing less than the weapon of a madman Inspector Lestrade."

The Oxford Don

Chapter 13 - The Dying Man

A few hours later we were at Newgate Prison as poor Inspector Lestrade, very much against his better judgment, had permitted Professor Findley to see his old friend one last time.

He only required that we not draw nearer to the dying man than the door. So there we found ourselves, a stout constable with a lantern before us and Lestrade beside us.

Professor Findley stared into the shadowy cell for some minutes in silence before DeGreystoke, in his fevered condition, realized he was no longer alone with his ghosts.

He rose up unsteadily upon one elbow and returned the gaze in silence. The flamboyant beard had been removed and a pale, sallow face stared out at us uncomprehendingly. Then, to the surprise of all gathered, the man spoke lucidly.

"Malcolm, my dear friend, I am approaching that dark valley we once spoke of, where all the paths meet and yet you live."

"I do," said the Oxford Don, compassionately, "and I shall go on living, despite your efforts."

Then, in a violent convulsion which twisted DeGreystoke's features into a mask of agony and hatred, he stretched out his hand and screamed.

"I shall sit at your table, visible only to thee!
I shall haunt thy steps, as your own shadow.
You, least deserving and most blessed, I hated.
Yet I, like Rome, lay dying...by my own hand!"

After this the man went limp and collapsed,

again unconscious to all around him.

"Come Professor," Lestrade insisted, "there is nothing more to be gained here."

With that we turned away and Holmes took the old man's arm into his own and led him off.

"That was a mistake Dr. Watson," Lestrade whispered, as we followed a little behind.

"I think not Inspector. Professor Findley has resisted accepting this devil's true nature. Those last words should cement it for him, once and for all, that Fitzwilliam DeGreystoke was a most evil man even to his very end."

The following day we saw Holmes' old tutor off at the station, but after our final goodbyes the diminutive figure grabbed me by the arm.

"I once asked you if you would publish the story of this case Dr. Watson, but I now believe that the downfall of Fitzwilliam DeGreystoke is the more fitting subject of a Shakespearean tragedy than one of your mysteries. Perhaps you might wait until my own departure before you take up your pen."

Holmes was especially introspective after the train for Oxford pulled away from the station and I did not intrude upon his thoughts. The Case of the Oxford Don was all but closed and yet there was a clear absence of the usual air of satisfaction which Holmes' generally exuded at such times. He returned to his chemical experiments as if there had been no interruption to them and I went to arranging my case notes while matters remained fresh in my mind.

We received two telegrams that evening. One

from the Oxford Don declared exuberantly that he had arrived safely at home and wished for nothing more than to never see the inside of a traveler's trunk again. He noted that Dean Liddell had voiced his wish that the College might extend some suitable kind of formal recognition for Holmes' services.

Meanwhile we were told that Mrs. Malcolm Findley wished to hold a soiree in our honor and her first question was to ask which date worked best for Mr. Sherlock Holmes.

The second telegram was from good Lestrade, who was keeping us abreast the developments with Mr. DeGreystoke. He said that the man's condition had weakened noticeably and he had remained delirious the entire day.

"He calls out curses against Findley one minute and entreaties with tears for forgiveness from his dead brother the next."

"How much longer can DeGreystoke go on, Watson?" Holmes asked at last.

He had not spoken upon the subject for nearly twenty-four hours but I could tell the situation was weighing upon his mind.

"I'm amazed he's held on this long," said I. "I've expected to receive the report of his passing with every hour. I fear that the fire of hatred is the only power keeping him alive now."

"Yes," Holmes said, mysteriously, then returned to his labors.

An hour later I looked up from my desk and found my friend staring intently at me.

"What is it?" I asked.

"I would very much like you to confirm the death of DeGreystoke, once we receive the news."

"Of course," I replied, for I was willing enough. "I shall inform Lestrade in the morning."

"I don't think you'll need to wait that long," he replied oddly, and then the bell rang. "I heard the carriage wheels grind upon the curb," said he.

Even as he'd appeared focused upon his work he had remained keenly alert and now he'd deduced that Lestrade was at our door. When the Inspector entered the look of relief upon his face was obvious.

"Well Gentlemen," said he, "that's it then."

"He's gone?" I asked.

"The evil genius is no longer in the land of the living. Our man declared him dead an hour ago and he now lies cold upon a slab."

"Holmes would like me to examine the body," I said, choosing not to use Holmes' actual words about confirming the findings of the Yard's man.

"That is easy enough if you can return with me."

"What do you suspect Mr. Holmes?" Lestrade asked as we approached the morgue.

"I suspect myself of jumping to conclusions," said he with a chuckle, "and I want to make sure that we are actually standing upon firm ground."

These last words were enough to allow both of us to deduce Holmes' fears for ourselves.

"You suspect the man of one last trick Mr. Holmes, but I can assure you that he is as dead as any corpse I've ever seen."

"It would be devilishly clever though," I willingly admitted, "and it would take the cooperation of only a very few to pull off such a thing."

"Two men Watson, to be exact. Between the physician and the mortician the thing could be seen to without the least disturbance and little risk to them."

"And once the grave was taken care of, who would there ever be to doubt the thing?" I asked.

"You've grasped it perfectly," Holmes replied, happily. "This is the final gambit which we must put down Watson."

Now I understood Holmes' intention. It wasn't enough to have a physician's word upon the death of such a man, nor a mortician's pledge that the body was buried in a certain place. It was necessary to see it all ourselves. Only then would we know.

I admit that once I comprehended the possibility of what DeGreystoke might have planned, I felt a strange knot in my stomach. The man had played us move-for-move across the country and had come within miles of reaching open water and the very real promise of freedom upon the continent. What more dramatic way to escape us forever than by staging his own death and then rising, by all appearances, from the grave?

Lestrade pulled the sheet back and a man's lifeless, gray face lay before us.

Holmes and I stood and looked together upon the corpse in silence.

"It is him!" Lestrade declared emphatically. He entertained no doubts.

"Is that him?" Holmes asked, although I was certain he knew for himself that it was DeGreystoke.

"It is," I answered, "but how strange the skin appears."

"What are you saying?" the Inspector cried out.

"Only that the skin almost appears to be wax," Holmes answered cooly.

"Wax! It can't be...wax!"

Inspector Lestrade grabbed for a surgical blade upon a nearby table and plunged it straight down into the corpse, driving it all the way in. Then he peered down into the flesh.

"There, you can see for yourselves Gentlemen," he almost screamed, the tension was so great. "It is a real man, our man! Fitzwilliam DeGreystoke is dead and there is no doubt about that Mr. Holmes."

"You're quite right Inspector," Holmes agreed, "Fitzwilliam DeGreystoke is...dead."

We took a hansom back to Baker Street and I asked Holmes if he'd truly suspected the devil of escaping.

"I did Watson," he admitted. "After everything we've endured it seemed a fitting, final move from the chess master. In the end the man we'd imbued with the power of a fiend turned out to be a mortal man after all. His brilliance had seen him through so much, but he could not escape the death he had intended for Professor Findley."

"Justice was done," I noted.

"Indeed my good fellow, but it was a close-run thing...and hard fought."

That evening Holmes took up his violin and Baker Street enjoyed an undisturbed evening of wonderful music wafting out the open windows of 221B.

The day was June 10th and I met my old friend, Stamford, at the Criterion Bar the next afternoon to discuss the sporting news. It had been the Criterion where we'd run into each other several years earlier when he'd told me about a fellow named Sherlock Holmes, who was looking to share rooms.

"What do you think of that Watson?" said he as he threw a fresh edition upon the table and leaned over, pointing with his finger.

"MT. TARAWERA ERUPTS," I read aloud.

"Yesterday," he said, "in New Zealand. A real catastrophe."

I said nothing but I felt it fitting that the death of a man like DeGreystoke, who was filled with such hatred, would correspond with one of the most cataclysmic events in the natural world.

A month later we were the honored guests of Dean Liddell, Professor and Mrs. Malcolm Findley, and the faculty of Christ Church College, Oxford.

"Welcome Mr. Holmes," someone in the crowd around us said.

"It is such an honor to meet you Dr. Watson, we love your stories," Mrs. Amitas Findley remarked, holding my hand.

The sea of friendly, smiling faces was nearly overwhelming for me and I knew they would be too much for my friend, but just then I beheld the face of Professor Findley. He was staring into the shadows under the arched wings of the dining room and it appeared he'd seen a...ghost.

After feasting, a round of songs by a ladies group, and several speeches, Holmes was finally called to the dais to be honored. He was then and asked to pull a velvet sheet from off some hidden form standing there next to him.

He obeyed without much emotion and very soon he was staring at his own likeness, cast in a white plaster bust and wearing the robes of a Roman Senator.

Thus the case of the Oxford Don was officially closed. As we moved the bust of my friend into a prominent place in our sitting room, the name of Fitzwilliam DeGreystoke vanished without even a mention in the papers and his body too, to an unmarked grave in an obscure Police Yard. Save for a few lines his name died with him.

The End

Thank you for reading:
"The Oxford Don"

What's next for Holmes & Watson?

Ranulf Briquessart, Viscount Briquessart of Rutledge, was dead. This truth was as undeniable as the noonday sun. Tragically his death had been preceded by that of his wife, a beauty of the Castilian nobility who was descended from the ancient Counts of Castile. It was sadly followed by the death of his only son, even before the honors and titles could be bestowed.

Now there was a card upon the table at 221B Baker Street from Lady Magdalena, the last surviving child of Sir Ranulf. The recently elevated Viscountess Briquessart requested the presence of Mr. Sherlock Holmes and Dr. John Watson at her Mayfair address.

"I'm afraid we must go Watson," Holmes said.

The De Briquessart Family stretched back to 1074 and the original Viscount Ranulf de Briquessart, so named for his Norman castle of Briquessart-en-Livry.

Such was the stature of the lady who now called upon Holmes and Watson, but little did they then realize that a mystery as dark and twisted as any they'd ever known was awaiting them out upon the Isles of Scilly.

"I shall die upon those islands Mr. Holmes; I know it. Will you help me?" the lady in the black mantilla begged.

Those words had so often brought Sherlock Holmes back into the fray and once again the game is afoot.

The Lady in the Black Mantilla!

Sherlock Holmes
The Lady in the Black Mantilla

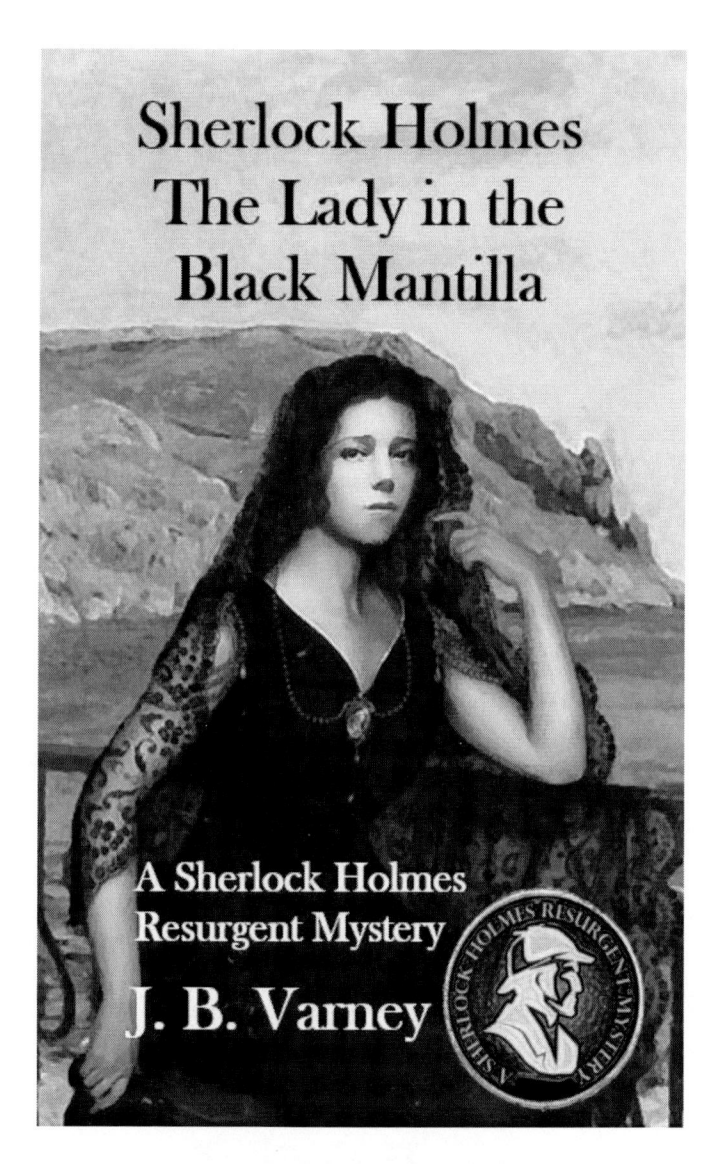

A Sherlock Holmes Resurgent Mystery

J. B. Varney

COMING SOON

The Sherlock Holmes
Resurgent Mysteries
by J. B. Varney

Elegy for a Baskerville
The Dreadnought Murders
The Deadly Cleric
The Tenth Man
The Constant Correspondent
The Oxford Don
The Lady in the Black Mantilla
Coming Soon

available at amazon.com

ABOUT THE AUTHOR

J. B. Varney "discovered" Sherlock Holmes as a boy. It was a time when none of his peers had read even one of Sir Arthur Conan Doyle's mysteries and thus began his life-long love of mystery and twisting plots.

Mr. Varney is a historian, genealogist, and descendant of many of the ancient families of Britain whose names grace the pages of his Sherlock Holmes mysteries.

"The game is... still afoot!"

Made in United States
North Haven, CT
23 March 2025